Journey to the Sky

Welcome to "Journey to the Sky," a narrative where the rugged landscape of the American West meets the innovative spirit of a burgeoning new age. In these pages, you will embark on a thrilling adventure that weaves together the classic elements of a Western drama while touching on the imaginative flair of steampunk.

Our story follows the resilient and resourceful Jedidiah Davenport, a ranch owner whose resolve is tested by the encroaching interests of a powerful railroad company. Amidst a backdrop of cattle ranches and open skies, Jedidiah's struggle symbolizes the timeless conflict between the indomitable spirit of individualism and the relentless march of industrial progress.

As you delve into the chapters, you will encounter a tapestry of characters - from the enigmatic Phineas with his outlandish inventions to the shadowy figures maneuvering behind the scenes of a rapidly changing world. Each character adds a unique thread to the rich narrative, creating a story that is as much about personal resilience and friendship as it is about the clash of old and new worlds.

"Journey to the Sky" also offers an imaginative twist to the traditional Western genre. The introduction of steampunk elements - airships, innovative machinery, and other anachronistic technologies - infuses the story with a sense of wonder and possibility. This blend of the historical and the fantastical invites you to imagine the Old West not just as it was, but as it might have been.

This novel is for those who love the thrill of adventure, the complexity of human struggles, and the joy of exploring imagined worlds. Whether you are a fan of Westerns, a lover of historical fiction, or simply someone who appreciates a good story, there is something in these pages for you.

So saddle up and prepare for a journey that will take you beyond the horizons of the ordinary, into a sky filled with adventure, intrigue, and the endless possibilities of the human spirit.

There, on the floor, lay Phineas B. Hargroves!

Journey to the Sky

A Jedidiah Davenport Adventure

BY PAUL EDWARD TURNER

Contents

Chapter		Page
I	THE MIDNIGHT STAMPEDE	1
II	A TOWN UNDER PRESSURE	15
III	THE BLASTED TRUTH	29
IV	CROSSROADS OF CONSPIRACY	43
V	UNSEEN BOUNDARIES	59
VI	BETRAYALS AND SECRET DEALS	75
VII	BLUEPRINTS OF DEFIANCE	91
VIII	A TWIST OF FATE	107
IX	PERILS IN THE SKY	121
X	SECURING THE FUTURE	135
XI	SHADOWS OF DOUBT	151
XII	FROM THE ASHES RISE	165
XIII	THE CELEBRATION	181
XIV	THE MAIDEN VOYAGE	193
XV	SHADOWS OF BETRAYAL	207
XVI	THE INVESTIGATION	221
XVII	THE WITNESS	237
XVIII	THE FINAL REVELATION	253
XIX	THE ESCAPE	267
XX	A NEW BEGINNING	283

CHAPTER I

The Midnight Stampede

"Stampede!" a terrified rancher screamed at the top of his lungs. "Stampede!" he continued to shout as over three hundred head of cattle stormed past him.

Inside the bunkhouse, a short distance away, over a dozen cattlemen were scrambling to their feet. In a flurry of movement, they sprang from their beds and hastily threw on their clothes. As they raced out the door, they passed the man who had sounded the alarm. He was still clanging a metal triangle. With no time to spare, each one hurried to the corral and saddled their horses.

"You men, go this way!" a tall, lanky cowboy shouted orders to a few of them. "You men, go that way!" he shouted to a few others. By the way he took command of the situation, it was obvious that he was the foreman of the ranch. "The rest of you, come with me!" he shouted to the remaining cowboys.

Shouts and hollers echoed as all the men spurred their horses, each galloping off in their assigned directions. It didn't take them long to overtake the stampeding cattle. They were headed in a direct path towards the ranch owner's house.

The ranch was owned by Jedidiah Davenport, a young man who had proven himself early in life by taking control of his father's one-horse freight company and turning it into a thriving business. At this point, he had added over two dozen freight offices, each boasting a minimum of four wagons. As his business profits grew, he invested wisely in land and cattle. He was now overseeing more than ten thousand acres and a thousand head of steer.

At this particular moment, the young entrepreneur was sitting in his office going over his financial ledgers. He was calculating the numbers in his books by the light of an oil lamp sitting on his desk. Suddenly, his thoughts were interrupted by the thunderous sound of hooves. The sounds of frightened cattle bellowing in the moonlight immediately told him what was going on.

The young man raced to his window and looked out just in time to see almost a third of his herd stampeding down the hill, straight towards his home. Luckily, he also saw a dozen or so men racing ahead of the cattle. They managed to position themselves between the house and the rampaging animals, firing their guns into the air. The loud blasts successfully diverted the cattle's path. Tragically, the only direction left to turn them was towards Davenport's garden, destroying all the produce growing there.

Jedidiah turned on his heel and dashed out of the room. He raced down the stairs to the main floor. He was met by his servants who had been woken from their sleep.

"What's going on, Mr. Davenport?" Agatha Porter asked as she tucked a lock of her gray hair behind her head. She had taken down the bun she normally wore it in.

"Something or someone stampeded the cattle!" Davenport responded, furiously.

"Land o' Goshen!" Pat Bennington exclaimed as he tugged at his suspenders. In his rush to find out what was going on, he had barely managed to throw on a pair of pants over his long underwear. "Did anyone get hurt?"

"I have no idea!" Jedidiah replied, glancing toward the front door. "From the looks of it, every man on this ranch is out trying to stop the stampede."

Agatha Porter pulled her house coat tighter around herself, keeping her arms folded in front. The chill in the night air didn't agree with her. "Did you say that something stampeded the cattle?"

"Something or someone..." Davenport stated

once again as he began walking towards the front entrance. Opening the door, he spotted a sheet of paper nailed to it that confirmed his suspicions. "Give in to the railroad, or next time it will be your whole herd!"

"Well, at least it was signed a friend!" Pat Bennington laughed to himself, as he glanced at Agatha Porter. The latter merely rolled her eyes and shook her head in disgust.

As the night's excitement finally settled and the ranch found a brief peace in the late hours, the first hints of dawn began to touch the sky. Inside the ranch house, the night's events lingered heavily in the air, setting a somber tone for the coming day.

****

Later that morning, Jedidiah found himself sitting at the kitchen table. He had just been served his usual breakfast of bacon and eggs when his foreman, Jim Davis, walked in.

"It took most of the night, but we finally managed to settle down the herd and get them back onto the grazing land." The tall man announced as he helped himself to a cup of the fresh coffee sitting on the stove beside him.

Jedidiah took a knife, cut open a steaming hot biscuit, and began to spread butter in the middle of it. He motioned for his hired man to have a seat at

"Give in to the railroad, or next time
it will be your whole herd!"

the table and join him. "Pat, fix Jim a plate!"

As Jim was sitting down, he commented, "I don't think what happened last night was an accident!"

Davenport responded by motioning towards the paper lying on the table. "I know it wasn't..."

"Next time it will be your whole herd!!!" Jim Davis shouted after grabbing the parchment. He clutched it in his firm grip. "This is all because you won't sell that section of land to the railroad!"

"That section of land would split this ranch in half," Jedidiah remarked, as he unfolded the napkin in front of him.

"I agree, selling the land is unreasonable and out of the question." The foreman fumed as he hastily pointed to the paper. "You need to let me round up the boys and hunt down whoever is responsible for this!"

"And where will you start?" Jedidiah asked curiously. "As far as I know this note is the only clue we have."

"I know how we can find out!" Pat Bennington glanced up from the stove.

"Oh?" Jedidiah Davenport turned towards his cook and waited for his response.

"It's a surefire plan!" Bennington smiled. "The dirty skunk signed it. So we know it was one of your friends. Tomorrow night, we throw a big shindig and invite everyone you know. Now they won't suspect me, so I'll just mosey up to each one of them and compliment the swell job they did on the cattle. If they thank me, we know it was them!" Pat laughed out loud as he looked back and forth between the two men.

"Pat..."

"I know, I know..." he chuckled. "Stick to my day job!" Pat turned around and began dishing up a serving of bacon and eggs for Jim Davis.

"You know as well as I do it was some hired thugs sent by Elijah Perkins to force you into signing that contract!" The foreman slammed the paper on the table.

"It could also have been any number of the business owners in town that stand to profit from the railroad." Jedidiah countered. "I heard they had a meeting yesterday to discuss how they could convince me to sell my land."

"So you want to just sit here and do nothing?" Jim Davis continued to grow more outraged. "I know this is your ranch and your decision but this also affects the lives of everyone that works for you!"

"Which is why I plan to ride into town and show this note to Sheriff Thompson!" Jedidiah stated as he prepared to eat the food in front of him. "I was already planning to go anyway. Pat gave me a list of supplies to get."

With a determined look, Jim Davis stood up and

pushed his chair back just as Pat Bennington was setting his plate down. His voice was firm, edged with resolve. "Well, I'm not going to just sit around and do nothing," he declared. Locking eyes with Jedidiah, he said, "I'm going to order the men to patrol every inch of the ranch. The moment there's any hint of trouble, I want them racing back to the bunkhouse. We need to be prepared for anything." As he said this, he turned on his heel and headed towards the door.

"What about your grub?" Pat called out as he motioned towards the meal he had just prepared.

"I've lost my appetite!" The foreman shouted as he stormed out.

Pat glanced back at his employer to see his reaction, just in time to see Davenport exiting the kitchen in the opposite direction. Chuckling to himself, the plump cook sat down at the table. He pulled the uneaten plate of bacon and eggs over in front of him and began buttering a biscuit for himself. "It's a good thing I made these just the way *I* like them!"

Having left the kitchen without his breakfast, Jedidiah Davenport spent a few moments reflecting on the night's events. Realizing that time was of the essence, he gathered his papers, secured his hat, and stepped out into the bright morning sun, ready to seek answers in town.

****

Nearly an hour later, Jedidiah was seen riding into Spoon Fork in his supply wagon. There were only a few men standing on the streets. Upon spotting the ranch owner, they immediately retreated into the local tavern known as The Rusty Nail Saloon. Davenport didn't think anything about this at the time. He pulled his wagon up in front of the general store and went inside.

"I'll be right with you!" The dark-haired man in the back room called out upon hearing the chime of the bell mounted above the entrance.

"Take your time. It's only me, Hank." Jedidiah responded to his long-time friend. "Pat sent me with a list of supplies."

Upon recognizing his voice, the store owner came rushing out of the back room. He appeared to be extremely nervous. "Jed... Oh... Hi... Now's not a good time, I'm about to close up for the day. You can leave your list, but you need to come back another time."

"Is anything wrong?" Jedidiah was confused as to why the man he had been doing business with for years was suddenly acting so frightened. It wasn't like Henry Porter to close up early on a weekday.

"Nothing's wrong, I just suddenly decided to

take a trip..."

"A trip?"

"I'm going fishing..."

"Don't you normally close early on Saturdays so you can spend the weekend down by the creek?" Davenport was growing suspicious.

"Fish wasn't biting this past weekend so I thought they might have gone on vacation..." Porter started pulling down the shades over his windows and door. "They might be back by now..."

"Well, aren't you afraid they might be in school during the week?" Jedidiah chuckled.

"In school..." Henry Porter thought for a second before it dawned on him. "Say that's not bad... Well, too bad I can't stick around... Got to get to school... I mean to the creek..."

"Hank, the list isn't long." Jedidiah began to get more serious. "I've got to go see the Sheriff. You could be gathering everything while I'm across the street. I'll be back in a few minutes. Then you can go..."

"I don't have time!" Henry Porter insisted, opening the door and motioning for Davenport to leave. "You know how I am about hunting. I like to be there before the crack of dawn."

"It's already nine o'clock in the morning and you said you were going..." Jedidiah suddenly cut his sentence short as he heard the sound of numerous boots approaching.

"I don't think you're understanding..." The leader of the group spoke up. "The proprietor is closing and you need to leave!"

"I didn't realize you had so many business partners, Hank..." Jedidiah remarked calmly, as he turned back towards the storekeep.

"Well, what can I say?" The dark-haired man replied nervously. "They know how much I was looking forward to this trip..."

Noticing the expressions on the faces of the eight men surrounding him, Jedidiah decided it would be best to go somewhere else. That's when he spotted Gideon Stewart standing in the crowd. Gideon owned the other general store in town.

"Gideon I normally do business with Hank, but I guess I can trade with you today," Jedidiah stated, casually.

The man in question started to respond but instead looked at the leader of the mob for permission. The latter merely stared back at him.

"Nothing personal, Jed..." The older man began to speak nervously. "I'm closing early today too. I'm going with Hank. I would stay but it's not every day you get to go shoot buffalo. Again, it's nothing personal..."

"Then why does it feel so personal?" Jedidiah remarked as he turned back towards Henry Porter. "You said you were going fishing."

Before he could respond, Gideon Stewart

suddenly shouted, "Doggone you, Hank! You know we decided to make it buffalo hunting!"

"I panicked..." Porter stammered. "Besides everybody knows I'm more of a fisherman than a hunter..."

"My guess is neither of you are going anywhere and this has something to do with me not selling my land to the railroad..." Jedidiah suddenly realized half of the men in the group were business owners in Spoon Fork. Those specific men were all standing with their heads down. They appeared to have a sense of shame as to what they were doing.

"I think you have guessed correctly!" The leader of the group replied sternly. "My name is Leroy Johnson and I represent Elijah Perkins of the D.&R.W. Railroad." As he made this statement, he reached into his pocket and produced a bill of sale.

"Gideon, Luther, Jacob, Horace..." The ranch owner ignored the antagonizer and addressed the men he had known for years. "Somebody stampeded my cattle last night and left a note on my door. I don't suppose any of you know anything about it?" Turning back towards Henry Porter, he asked, "What about you, Hank?"

"Nobody got hurt... Did they, Jed?" The store owner asked genuinely concerned.

Before Davenport could respond, the ring leader grabbed him by the shoulder and spun him around. He shoved the bill of sale into his chest and said,

"Unless you're ready to do business, I think you should get back in your wagon and head home."

"What if I choose not to?" Jedidiah Davenport asked unwilling to move.

The man who was more than twice Jedidiah's size leaned down into his face. "I guess you'll just have to find out..."

Suddenly remembering the rifle lying on the seat of his supply wagon, Jedidiah unexpectedly shoved the man into the crowd behind him. This cleared a path for Davenport who made a mad dash for it.

"Get him!" The angry man shouted as he and the three others he landed on struggled to stand up. The business owners didn't know what to do. Davenport brushed past them rather easily.

The young ranch owner had just leaped onto his wagon and grabbed his rifle when he heard a gunshot. This was immediately followed by a second blast. Whirling around he spotted three newcomers. Two of them had forty-five caliber pistols ready to use. The third man was reloading his double-barrel shotgun.

"Hold it, right there!" The newcomer man shouted, as he leveled his weapon and prepared to fire a third time.

CHAPTER II

A Town Under Pressure

"Put that rifle down, Jed!" the older man shouted, maintaining a firm grip on his shotgun.

"Sheriff Thompson!" Jedidiah breathed a sigh of relief and immediately did as instructed.

Sheriff Thompson, a figure of authority and wisdom in Spoon Fork, stepped forward, his demeanor calm yet commanding. With years of experience etched into the lines of his face, he was a man who had seen much and learned more. His sharp eyes surveyed the scene with an understanding born of countless encounters like this one.

"I want everybody to break this up and go back to their respective places of business!" The older man directed these commands directly to the business leaders of Spoon Fork. Turning his attention towards the large man who had incited the riot he said, "Johnson, I told you not to start any trouble in my town!"

"Not starting any trouble, Sheriff," he replied nonchalantly. "Just trying to help Davenport see the value of a good business deal!"

"I've already told Elijah Perkins that I have no intention of splitting my ranch in half!" Jedidiah stated in a firm voice. "You can tell him that again. He's going to have to find another way around!"

"Mister Perkins has already offered you twice what that land is worth!" Johnson retorted as if he didn't understand what the issue was. "He's now willing to go to three times the value!"

"Not even at a thousand times the value is it worth it to me to divide my grazing land in two!" The Ranch Owner began to grow more outraged. "If you think stampeding my herd is going to make me change my mind, you're quite mistaken!"

"Is this true, Johnson?" Sheriff Thompson spoke up. "Did you stampede Davenport's cattle?"

"Of course not!" The large man replied. "We couldn't do anything like that. We've been here in town all night, playing hopscotch on the sidewalk!" He immediately burst into laughter as well as his three cronies.

"All right, I've heard enough!" Sheriff Thompson exclaimed as he pointed towards the saloon. "Johnson take your men and crawl back into the bottle you crawled out of!" Turning his attention to Jedidiah, he stated. "Unless Davenport wants to press harassment charges."

"Actually, that's what I came into town to talk to you about, Sheriff." The ranch owner replied as he reached inside his shirt pocket and pulled out a folded-up sheet of paper. "Whoever stampeded my cattle..." He looked directly at Johnson, "left this for a calling card." Jedidiah held up the note for all to see. He was just about to hand it over to Sheriff Thompson when someone snatched it away.

"Give in to the railroad or next time it will be your whole herd," Johnson read aloud, then added with a smirk, "Sounds like some good advice, Davenport!"

"Let me see that..." Sheriff Thompson stated, as he reached over and took the paper away from Johnson. After reading the note himself, he looked at the large man again and said, "I've asked you once. Now I'm gonna ask you for the last time! Did you have anything to do with this?"

"Sheriff that would be against the law and I wouldn't consider doing anything against the law..." Johnson remarked with a mock look of innocence on his face.

"Besides, it was signed 'a friend,'" one of Johnson's cronies spoke up. He chuckled as he added, "He and Davenport definitely ain't friends!"

"That's right!" the ring leader agreed. "We're not friends. I just like to offer friendly advice, like advising you to take Mister Perkins' offer."

"I've done just fine without your advice up till now!" Davenport retorted. "I thank you to keep your opinions to yourself. Friendly or not."

"Okay, that's enough." Sheriff Thompson spoke up as he ordered his two deputies to escort Johnson and his men back to The Rusty Nail.

After they walked away, Sheriff Thompson invited Davenport inside. The sheriff's office, nestled within the small town of Spoon Fork, was a modest structure, befitting the simplicity of the town it served. The walls were lined with wanted posters and local ordinances, and a sturdy desk sat in the center, cluttered with papers and reports. Across the room from the desk were two cells, their bars a stark reminder of the consequences of breaking the law in this seemingly peaceful town. In one corner stood a potbelly stove, its gentle brewing of coffee offering a comforting presence amidst the seriousness of the office. The room was imbued with a sense of order and a trace of the countless stories and confessions it had witnessed.

"Care for a cup of coffee?" Sheriff Thompson graciously offered his guest.

"No thanks," Jedidiah politely declined. "I didn't come for a social call. I came to show you that note and see about getting some justice!"

Sheriff Thompson poured himself a cup of coffee as he casually asked "What do you want me to do about it?"

Outraged, Jedidiah shouted, "Over three hundred head of my cattle were stampeded last night and it says next time it will be the whole herd. I want Johnson and his men arrested!"

"Where's your proof?" Sheriff Thompson asked as he sat down behind his desk.

"That note is my proof!" Jedidiah exclaimed. "Johnson nailed it to my front door last night while he and his men were stampeding my cattle!"

"Did you see Johnson or any of his men write the note?"

"Well not exactly..."

"Did you see Johnson or any of his men nail it to your door?"

"Well not exactly..."

Sighing reluctantly, Sheriff Thompson said, "Then unfortunately my hands are tied!"

"Of course they are!" Jedidiah was fuming by this point. "What about Porter and Stewart refusing to sell to me? I can't operate my ranch without supplies!"

"There's no law saying they have to do business with you," Sheriff Thompson remarked, deep in thought. "In fact, I think there's a law stating a private business has the right to refuse service to anyone..." The older man then began pulling open several desk drawers, searching for something. Finally finding a law book, he started thumbing through it just as Jedidiah spoke up again.

"What about the mob that formed in the street and surrounded me?" The ranch owner was growing more outraged by the moment.

"Did any of them touch you?" The Sheriff asked as he closed the book and returned it to the drawer.

"Johnson put his hands on me!"

"And then you shoved him into his men, knocking them all to the ground..." The older man stated matter-of-factly. "My deputies and I saw you from across the street as we were walking over. Actually, Johnson has more cause to press charges than you do."

"It was self-defense!"

"Maybe a jury would see it that way, maybe they wouldn't..."

"You know as well as I do, Elijah Perkins hired Johnson and his group of outlaws to force me into selling my land!"

"Never said he didn't..." Sheriff Thompson remarked causally. "However, I've got to look at it from the standpoint of the law. We've got to have proof."

"So in the meantime, I just sit back and let these men get away with whatever they want?"

"They'll eventually slip up." Sheriff Thompson stated confidently. "That's when we'll get them." Glancing in the general direction of the street, he remarked, "For example, did you notice one of Johnson's men knew the note was signed a friend?"

Jedidiah snapped his fingers as it dawned on him! "When Johnson read the note aloud he stopped before he got to that part!"

"From where the other man was standing, he couldn't possibly have seen what was written on the paper." The Sheriff added confidently. "Just take my advice, let the law do its job."

"What about the crop I lost due to the stampede?"

"As soon as we have proof, we can charge them with damages."

"Sheriff, just so you know, I have no intention to ever sell my land," Jedidiah stated with conviction. "No matter what Perkins and his men do to me."

Sheriff Thompson leaned back in his chair and calmly said, "You don't have to. The law is on your side." He thought for a second and added, "Although the railroad coming through would be good for the valley. It'd make a lot of folks around these parts happy."

"Are you trying to get me to sell now too?" Jedidiah asked shocked.

Never changing his tone or attitude, the Sheriff stated, "Now calm down, boy. I've got no stake in this matter other than maintaining peace and order and abiding by the letter of the law."

"I just thought you were saying..."

"I was saying the law is on your side!"

"That's comforting..." Jedidiah remarked sarcastically.

"Eventually Perkins, Johnson, or one of their men will slip up." Sheriff Thompson paused to take another drink of coffee, before saying, "may I make a suggestion?"

"Let me guess..." Jedidiah sighed as he rolled his eyes and asked "Let the law handle this?"

"Well actually, I was just going to suggest wiring one of your other freight offices, have them pick up your supplies, and ship them to you."

"Oh... why didn't I think of that?" Jedidiah's face suddenly lightened up and he laughed a little.

"Because you're not the Sheriff..." The older man chuckled. "No, you would have thought of it eventually. I just beat you to the punch."

Jedidiah reached into his pants and pulled out his pocket watch. "If I hurry I can get the supplies shipped out from Sheffield and have them here this afternoon."

"I think I'll walk over with you," Sheriff Thompson said as he stood up, then quickly added, "That is if you don't mind?"

"Considering the reception I've been given this morning, that might not be a bad idea!" Jedidiah agreed earnestly. He turned on his heel and led the way out into the dry, dusty streets of Spoon Fork.

A few minutes later, Jedidiah found himself stepping into the telegraph office run by Horace

McKinley. Horace, who had been among the businessmen with Johnson and his crew during the earlier confrontation, was a well-informed individual. As the operator of the town's telegraph, he often caught wind of any news or gossip first. This role made him meticulous, taking pride in keeping the town connected to the wider world.

Horace was finishing sending a telegraph when he heard Jedidiah step through the door. "I'll be right with you!" He announced without even looking up to see who it was.

"Take your time Horace!" Jedidiah replied as he walked closer to the busy individual.

Immediately recognizing the sound of his voice, Mr. McKinley nervously fumbled with the telegraph as he finished sending it. Finally, he reluctantly looked up. "Jed... about earlier..."

"Forget it..." Jedidiah cut him off before he could continue. "Johnson has you and the other men buffaloed into pressuring me into selling to the railroad."

"You gotta see it from our point of view, Jed!" Horace exclaimed. "Do you know how much business this could mean for the whole valley?"

"Do you know how it could split my entire ranch straight down the middle?"

"I heard they offered you a real good price!"

"My land isn't for sale!"

"I wish you'd change your mind..."

Mr. McKinley nervously fumbled with the
telegraph as he finished sending it.

"Horace!" Jedidiah cut him off again. "I just want to send a telegraph to my Sheffield freight office. I need them to gather some supplies and send them on the wagon coming back this evening."

"Jed I hate to tell you this but..."

"You refuse to send my telegraph?"

"Well, it just so happens that my telegraph is busted!" Horace motioned towards the machine in question. "If it wasn't for that I'd be happy to send it for you!"

A look of amusement came over Jedidiah's face and he said, "Weren't you sending a telegraph when I walked in?"

"That was just a test telegraph!" Horace McKinley started fidgeting around. "I was just sending nonsense trying to see if I'd get any response. I was actually sending Mary had a little lamb..."

Suddenly Sheriff Thompson revealed himself by stepping into the building. He walked over and stood next to Jedidiah Davenport. "Mary had a little lamb?" He reached over and picked up a paper lying on the desk in front of McKinley. After reading it over, he said, "You know I happen to know a little bit about Morse code and what you transmitted sounded more like what's written on this paper than a nursery rhyme."

Horace suddenly dropped his head in shame and

sighed deeply. "Alright, Sheriff, you caught me. The telegraph is working just fine." He took the paper from Sheriff Thompson and placed it back on the desk, his hands visibly shaking now. "I'll send your telegram, Jed."

Jedidiah watched as Horace reluctantly seated himself at the telegraph machine. He could feel the operator's anxiety with each tap, each pause, as if the very air had grown heavy with Horace's defeat.

The machine came to life, clicking and tapping as Horace relayed the message to Sheffield. Jedidiah didn't move and didn't speak until the final acknowledgment came through. Only then did he allow himself a small nod of satisfaction.

"Thank you, Horace," Jedidiah said sarcastically. Before turning on his heel to walk out of the shop, he tossed the money for the telegraph onto the desk. "Keep the change!" He called out as he stepped into the street. He was furious.

"I know you've got a right to be upset," the Sheriff tried to be a voice of reason, as he met up with the young entrepreneur. "Just try to remain calm and don't let it get to you!"

Jedidiah sighed and took a deep breath, saying, "I'm trying. I'm just lucky you know Morse code, or I wouldn't even be getting my supplies!"

"I don't know Morse code!"

Jedidiah suddenly looked confused. "But you just said..."

"I said I know a little bit *about* Morse code..." The Sheriff's face suddenly began to form a smirk. "I never said that I knew Morse code!"

Jedidiah stood dumbfounded for a moment before he began to laugh out loud. At least he still had one friend left in Spoon Fork. It was obvious that Sheriff Thompson was willing to help in any way he could, as long as it stayed within the limits of the law.

After parting ways with the Sheriff, Jedidiah decided to stroll over to the main branch of his freight company. Since this was where it had all begun, Jedidiah Davenport naturally decided to make Spoon Fork the headquarters for his empire.

As Jedidiah was approaching it, the early morning sun was casting a golden glow over the now bustling streets of Spoon Fork. The sign above the entrance proudly read, "Davenport Dispatch & Delivery," The building, where it all started, stood as a testimony of his hard work and ambition.

Jedidiah's steps quickened, fueled by a mix of pride and a pressing need to set things right after the morning's events. His hand reached for the door handle, ready to step into the familiar confines of his empire.

But in a split second, the calm of the morning was shattered. A deafening explosion erupted from within the building, the force of the blast hurling the door off its hinges and hurtling toward Jedidiah with terrifying speed.

Jedidiah's reflexes kicked in, but he was too late to escape the impact. The door slammed into him with brutal force, knocking him off his feet and sending him sprawling onto the dusty street!

CHAPTER III

The Blasted Truth

A cloud of smoke and debris billowed from the doorway, obscuring the interior. As the echo of the explosion faded, a stunned silence fell over Spoon Fork's main street. Townsfolk emerged from shops and homes, their faces etched with shock and concern. Amidst the chaos, Jedidiah lay dazed and disoriented, his mind racing to comprehend what had just happened.

The ringing in Jedidiah's ears was the only sound he could discern as he slowly pushed himself up from the dusty ground. His vision blurred, focusing slowly on the wreckage of what was once the proud entrance to his company's headquarters. The smell of gunpowder lingered in the air, mixing with the dust and debris that had settled around him.

People from the town began to gather, their murmurs growing louder as they approached the site of the explosion. "Jedidiah, are you alright?" someone called out, but their voice seemed distant, muffled by the ringing in his ears.

Struggling to his feet, Jedidiah brushed off his clothes, his eyes scanning the crowd for any sign of who might be responsible. The townsfolk's expressions shifted from concern to a mixture of fear and curiosity. They whispered among themselves, casting wary glances at the source of the explosion.

Sheriff Thompson pushed through the crowd, his face grim. "Jed, what happened here?" he demanded, his eyes searching the scene for clues.

"I wish I knew, Sheriff," Jedidiah replied, his voice steady despite the shock. "I was just about to enter when..." His voice trailed off as he looked at the remains of the door, now lying several feet away.

As the dust settled, Jedidiah's first thought was for the employees inside the building. His heart raced as he struggled to clear his vision, the aftermath of the explosion still ringing in his ears. "The office!" he exclaimed, a sense of urgency gripping him. "There are people inside!"

Sheriff Thompson, realizing the gravity of the situation, barked orders to the townspeople. "We need help here! Form a line, and be careful. We don't know if the structure's stable."

The townsfolk, spurred into action by the

Sheriff's commands, began organizing themselves. Some fetched water in case of fire, while others cautiously approached the damaged building to assess the situation and look for survivors.

Jim Davis, alongside Jedidiah, rushed towards the entrance, or what remained of it. "Jed, be careful!" Jim cautioned, but Jedidiah was already moving into the smoke-filled interior.

The scene inside was chaotic. Desks and paperwork were strewn everywhere, the explosion having turned the orderly office into a scene of disarray. Jedidiah called out, "Is anyone in here? Can you hear me?"

Groans and coughs responded from under the debris. Jedidiah and Jim, joined by a few brave townsfolk, began carefully removing pieces of wood and broken furniture, searching for the trapped employees.

They found the manager and dispatcher, Mr. Clayton, pinned under a fallen beam, conscious but with his leg trapped. "I'm here, Jed," he coughed, trying to push the debris off himself. "The others... I think they're over there," he gestured weakly towards the back of the office.

Working swiftly but carefully, Jedidiah and the others managed to free Mr. Clayton and three more employees. They were bruised and shaken, but alive. Relief was clearly shown on Jedidiah's face as each employee was accounted for and helped out of the building.

Outside, the townsfolk tended to the injured, offering water and makeshift bandages. Meanwhile, Sheriff Thompson was taking statements, trying to piece together what had happened.

The Sheriff turned to the gathering crowd. "Did anyone see anything? Anyone approaching the building before the blast?" The townsfolk exchanged glances, but no one spoke up.

Jedidiah's mind raced. This wasn't just an attack on his property; it was a blatant message! "Now will you have Johnson and his men arrested?"

"Do you have proof it was them?" Sheriff Thompson asked, sincerely. He turned to Mr. Clayton and asked him if he had seen Johnson or any of his men skulking about the office that morning.

"Gotta admit, I haven't seen any of them around and I've been here since five o'clock." Mr. Clayton reluctantly replied while the town doctor wrapped a bandage around his head.

"Any of you men?" Sheriff Thompson asked. They all admitted to not seeing anyone in the freight office who shouldn't have been there.

Suddenly Leroy Johnson himself stepped out of the crowd of spectators and said, "Sheriff, we had nothing to do with that explosion. We've been in the Rusty Nail ever since it opened this morning."

Glancing over at Jedidiah, he quickly added, "Except for the brief meeting we had with Mr. Davenport when we offered him that friendly advice..."

"You got proof you were there?" The Sheriff asked, in a demanding tone.

"He's telling the truth, Sheriff." Luther Caldwell owner of the Rusty Nail Saloon reluctantly stepped forward. "Mr. Johnson and his men have been at my place all morning. Except for the incident with Jed over at the general store."

Jedidiah with a look of worry stated, "We need to be on high alert. There's no way this could have been an accident. It was intentional sabotage!"

The Sheriff nodded gravely. "I'll get to the bottom of this, Jed. But you need to be careful. Whoever did this might not stop here."

Jedidiah looked back at the smoldering remains of his office, a mix of anger and determination settling in. This was no longer just a fight for his land; it was a fight for survival. And he was not about to back down.

"Sheriff, I want to at least find out where the explosion came from." The young entrepreneur stated with an air of determination. "It might help us figure out how Johnson and his men did it!"

Jedidiah, Sheriff Thompson, and Jim Davis cautiously reentered the charred remains of the Davenport Dispatch & Delivery office. The early morning sunlight filtered through the dust and debris, casting an eerie glow over the devastation. Amidst the wreckage, the trio began their search for clues.

"Be careful," the Sheriff warned, stepping gingerly over a pile of smoldering papers. "We don't know if this place is stable."

Jedidiah, his face a mask of concern, moved towards the overturned safe. "Perkins has gone too far," he murmured, his hands sifting through the debris. "He could have seriously injured one of the men working here. His beef is with me, not the people who work for me!"

Sheriff Thompson, always the voice of reason, said, "We still don't have any proof that it was him, Johnson, or any of his cronies."

"Who else could it have been?" Jedidiah asked, in disgust. He was still taking in the damage done to his freight office.

Jim, who was examining the scorched floors, called out, "Sheriff, come look at this." He pointed to a spot under where the safe had been as it was now blown off its foundation. "It looks like the explosion originated from here."

Sheriff Thompson knelt, analyzing the area. "It's possible this was an attempted robbery gone wrong," he suggested, "but given the recent tensions, I wouldn't rule out other motives."

Jedidiah's eyes narrowed. "A robbery? Here?"

The early morning sunlight filtered
through the dust and debris.

He shook his head in disbelief. "It doesn't add up. We rarely keep any money here, and everyone in town knows that."

Sheriff Thompson sifted through the debris near the safe and retrieved a damaged alarm clock. "This was set for ten thirty," he remarked.

Jedidiah's eyes narrowed. "That settles it! No robber would time an explosion for when the office is at its busiest. Like I said before, It was deliberate sabotage!"

The Sheriff met Jedidiah's gaze, his expression a mix of agreement and caution. "Agreed, but without proof, we're still in the dark."

A moment of silence followed, filled only by the distant murmur of the crowd finally dispersing outside. Jedidiah's thoughts were suddenly interrupted by the realization that Jim Davis, his foreman, was in town and not at his ranch. Jedidiah's gaze shifted to the tall lanky man. "Jim, why are you here? Shouldn't you be at the ranch overseeing things?" he asked.

Jim, taken aback by the abrupt question, hesitated. His hands fidgeted nervously before he responded, "Well, I... After I got the men organized, I thought it'd be better if I came to town. To make sure you were safe, Jed."

Jedidiah studied Jim's face intently. There was a tense pause before Jedidiah spoke again, his voice softer, "I appreciate that, Jim, but we need all hands at the ranch, especially now."

"I understand, Jed," Jim replied, his voice steadying. "I'll head back right away." He cast a final look around the ruined office before turning to leave, the weight of Jedidiah's unspoken suspicions hanging heavily in the air.

As Jim departed, Sheriff Thompson clapped a reassuring hand on Jedidiah's shoulder. "We'll get to the bottom of this, Jed. You have my word."

Jedidiah nodded, his gaze lingering on the doorway through which Jim had just exited. Deep in thought, he wondered about the explosion, the railroad, and the unsettling feeling that the troubles facing Davenport Dispatch & Delivery were far from over.

Almost in answer to his thoughts, Horace McKinley came rushing inside with a handwritten telegraph. "Jed this just came in over the wire. It's from your Sheffield freight office!"

Without thinking twice, Jedidiah reached out and jerked it from McKinley's hand. "It's from Matt!"

Matthew "Matt" Colton, Jedidiah's childhood friend and now the manager of the Sheffield branch of Davenport Dispatch & Delivery, was as close as family. Standing only a few inches taller than Jedidiah, Matt's presence was always felt more in his character than his stature. Known for his sharp wit and exceptional horsemanship, he was also a skilled marksman, respected throughout the region. He shared a bond with Jedidiah. Growing up together, they had journeyed through countless adventures, their friendship only strengthening with time. Now managing the Sheffield office, Matt combined efficiency with good-natured humor, making him a favorite among both clients and staff. His messages to Jedidiah often interwove business updates with playful reminiscences, maintaining the light-hearted camaraderie of their youth.

"What does he say, Jed?" Sheriff Thompson asked anxiously.

Jedidiah hastily folded the note and placed it in his shirt pocket before replying. "He says there's been trouble and wants me to ride out immediately!"

"I'll go with you!" Sheriff Thompson quickly volunteered. "Sheffield is out of my jurisdiction but you might run into trouble."

"No, I don't need you to leave town, Sheriff!" Jedidiah responded decisively. "I need you here to keep an eye on Johnson and his men. This may just be a ploy to get me out of the way."

"What about this office here?"

Jedidiah thought about this for a moment before saying, "Can you please go over to Doc's office and check on Mr. Clayton and my other employees? I need to know if they'll be able to come back to work today."

"Of course, but do you expect them to work in this mess?" The older man asked earnestly.

Jedidiah glanced around the room and said, "Good point! Do you think you could persuade one of your deputies to ride out to my ranch and relay a message to Jim?"

"What message do you want relayed?"

"I should have enough lumber and supplies in my barn to repair the damages," Jedidiah said. "Ask your deputy to tell Jim to gather a few of the men and bring what's needed to make this place workable again." Clenching his fists and tightening his jaw, his frustration was evident. "I should have told Jim this myself before I ordered him to ride out of town a few minutes ago."

"Well, you had a lot on your mind," Sheriff Thompson replied as reassuringly as possible. "Don't worry, Jed. You go check on your friend and your other branch. I'll see to it that everything is taken care of here."

Jedidiah, his thoughts a whirlwind of concern and resolve, swiftly made his way to where his supply wagon was parked in front of the general store. He hastily climbed aboard and steered it around to the back of the freight office. His movements were swift and decisive, each action a reflection of the urgency he felt.

After parking the wagon, he unhitched his sturdy chestnut horse, a reliable companion named

Blaze, with whom he had been through many journeys. The horse nickered softly, sensing the tension in the air. Jedidiah retrieved a saddle from the back room of the freight office and efficiently prepared his mount for the ride ahead.

With the saddle securely in place and his rifle resting in its holster, Jedidiah swung himself up. He took a brief moment to glance back at the chaotic ruins of his office, the sight fueling a deep-seated determination. His expression was a mix of resolve and concern, reflecting the weight of the morning's events and the urgency of the message from his friend Matt.

He spurred his horse into a steady gallop, leaving a cloud of dust swirling behind him as he rode out of town. The midday sun was high in the sky, casting a warm glow over the streets of Spoon Fork, contrasting sharply with the morning's events.

As he disappeared from view, a sense of unease lingered in the air. The town's main street, usually bustling with activity, seemed unusually quiet, the townsfolk watching Jedidiah's departure with a mix of curiosity and concern. The echo of his horse's hooves faded in the distance, leaving behind a sense of anticipation and uncertainty.

Just as the townsfolk began to disperse, a sudden, sharp cry pierced the air. "Wait! Look at this!" called out a deputy, holding up a metallic object found in the debris. The crowd halted, turning back with renewed interest. The deputy held the item aloft, and in the glaring midday sun, it glinted ominously, hinting at a clue possibly overlooked in the chaos.

CHAPTER IV

Crossroads of Conspiracy

The sun was high in the sky as Jedidiah Davenport rode into Sheffield. His horse, Blaze, lathered with sweat, its sides heaving slightly from the exertion of the twenty-five-mile journey. Jedidiah himself felt the fatigue of the ride, his body aching but his mind alert, fueled by a mixture of concern and determination.

Sheffield was a bustling town, smaller than Spoon Fork but lively in its own right. The streets were lined with a variety of shops and businesses, each contributing to the town's vibrant atmosphere.

Jedidiah directed his horse towards the Sheffield branch of Davenport Dispatch & Delivery. The building stood out with its well-kept façade and the familiar sign above the entrance. He dismounted with a sense of urgency, his boots kicking up small clouds of dust as he landed.

Tying his horse to a nearby post, Jedidiah

quickly made his way inside the office. The interior was a hive of activity, with employees bustling about, handling paperwork, and coordinating deliveries. At the sight of Jedidiah, the room fell into a hushed silence, a mixture of respect and concern etching the faces of his employees.

"Mr. Davenport, you're here!" exclaimed a young clerk, breaking the silence. "We weren't expecting you!"

"I came as fast as I could," Jedidiah replied, his gaze scanning the room. "Where's Matt? I got his message."

"Mr. Colton is in his office, sir," the clerk informed. His face formed an expression of confusion, as he began gesturing towards a door at the far end of the room.

Jedidiah wasted no time, striding towards the back office. As he opened the door, he found Matthew "Matt" Colton, his childhood friend and now manager of the Sheffield branch, poring over a stack of papers. Matt looked up, his face also a look of confusion.

"Jed, what are you doing here?" Matt asked, standing up. "I wasn't expecting you to visit for another month!"

"What are you talking about?" Jedidiah asked, his voice tense. "You sent me this telegraph and asked me to come right away!" Jedidiah reached into his shirt pocket and produced the handwritten note.

Matt's expression grew more confused as he took it from Jedidiah's hand. "I didn't send this!"

"You didn't?" Jedidiah was taken back in shock. "So I just rode almost three hours for nothing?"

"Not for nothing," Matt replied. "I'm actually glad you're here. We've been having trouble."

The young entrepreneur closed his eyes and took a deep breath before asking, "What kind of trouble?"

"It's the shipments, Jed. They've been tampered with. Several of our deliveries have been delayed or gone missing entirely. It's like someone's trying to choke our supply lines."

Jedidiah's brow furrowed, his suspicions confirmed. "Definitely Perkins' handiwork. He's escalating his tactics," he said. His expression then shifted to a mix of confusion and panic. "What exactly do you mean by gone missing entirely?"

"There's been three hold-ups over the past month alone." Matthew Colton reluctantly explained. Despite his long-time friendship with Jedidiah, he was still nervous to tell him about the robberies.

"Why am I just now hearing about this?" Jedidiah was outraged but quickly regained his composure. "Never mind, if this is happening to your office, there's no telling how many more of my offices it's happening to."

Matthew nodded grimly. "There's something else you need to see." He reached into his desk drawer and pulled out a small, battered package. "This was left at our doorstep early this morning."

Jedidiah took the package, turning it over in his hands. It was crudely wrapped, and there was no indication of its sender. Carefully, he untied the string and peeled back the paper. Inside was a small, intricately carved wooden figurine – a train, its features remarkably detailed.

"It's a message, Jed," Matthew said, watching Jedidiah closely. "Whoever's doing this is clearly connected to the railroad."

Jedidiah's grip tightened on the figurine, a surge of anger mingling with an uneasy sense of being watched and hunted. He looked up at Matt, his eyes hard with resolve.

"We need to strengthen our security, here, Spoon Fork, and all the other branches," Jedidiah declared.

Matt nodded in agreement. "I'll double the guards on our shipments and start asking around. Someone in town must know something."

Jedidiah placed the figurine back inside the package, his mind racing. "I'll head back to Spoon Fork with the wagon you're sending out with my supplies. We need to prepare for whatever comes next. Perkins is playing a dangerous game."

"Oh yes about that..." Matthew began to speak

but was interrupted abruptly by his friend.

"Don't tell me they wouldn't sell you my supplies either?" Jedidiah asked, dejectedly.

"Oh no, it's not that." Matthew Colton replied, confidently. "It's just that the drivers aren't going to be leaving for another hour yet. They're over at the Cobblestone Inn having a bite to eat."

Jedidiah's stomach suddenly began to rumble at the mere mention of food. It was getting close to four o'clock, and he hadn't had a bite to eat all day. He had left his breakfast sitting on the table back home and hadn't had a chance to eat anything since then.

"You sound like you could use some food yourself," Matthew remarked, hearing the rumble.

"Matt I'm so hungry I could eat a horse!" Jedidiah laughed heartily. "Care to join me for a steak?" Davenport paused for a moment as he noticed the slight hesitation on his friend's face. He quickly added, "My treat!"

"I've already had lunch and a big breakfast before that." Matthew reluctantly declined the offer. "I'll walk with you over there."

"Fair enough!" Jedidiah chuckled.

"But before we go, maybe we should check with the telegraph office," Matthew suggested. "We can find out who sent that message."

Jedidiah had become so distracted by his hunger that he had almost completely forgotten about the telegraph that had brought him there. "That's a good idea! I should have thought of that myself!"

The Sheffield telegraph office was just a stone's throw away. Inside, the lone operator, a middle-aged man with spectacles perched on his nose, was busily tapping away. Upon their inquiry, he looked up, baffled. "No, sirs, I didn't send that telegram to Spoon Fork. I've been here since dawn, and the only telegram I've sent was in response to your request for supplies."

Matt frowned, but Jedidiah, feeling the weight of his empty stomach, decided to set aside the mystery for now. "We'll look into this later, Matt. First, I need to grab something to eat."

Inside the Cobblestone Inn, Jedidiah chose a secluded table and ordered a hearty steak, hoping it would ease some of the day's stress. Matt excused himself, needing to return to the office. Left alone, Jedidiah's gaze wandered around the restaurant, landing on a newspaper left on the adjacent table. The headline grabbed his attention immediately. He picked up the paper and read it aloud, "Around the World in an Airship: A Modern Marvel."

Jedidiah was immediately captivated by the idea of an airship, a vessel not limited by the constraints of roads or rails. Amidst the ongoing challenges with Perkins and the railroad, this concept felt like a breath of fresh air, a potential solution to his transportation woes. As he waited for his steak, his mind buzzed with possibilities. Could an airship be the key to dealing with the railroad's control over land routes? The more he pondered, the more sense it made. An airship could offer a way to transport goods without relying on traditional methods, keeping his business running independently of Perkins' influence.

Lost in thought, Jedidiah barely noticed when his steak arrived. However, once he noticed its arrival, Jedidiah put all other thoughts out of his mind. He concentrated solely on the food in front of him, savoring every single bit of the steak, mashed potatoes, corn on the cob, and hot buttered biscuits.

Jedidiah had just finished the last bite when he looked up and saw two large men standing over him.

"Can I help you, gentlemen?" He asked slightly confused.

"As a matter of fact, you can!" one of them stated firmly, slamming down a bill of sale for his land. "Sign these papers and stop holding up the railroad!"

Jedidiah wiped his mouth with his napkin and laid it on the table. He very calmly asked, "Who sent you, Perkins or Johnson?"

"Our employer is our own affair!" The man gruffly retorted.

"I believe I've already made myself clear where

I stand on this matter." Jedidiah picked up his newspaper and slid his chair back from the table. "If you'll excuse me, gentleman, I have matters requiring my attention elsewhere."

"I think they can wait," the other man spoke up as he placed a hand on Jedidiah's shoulder. The first man placed a hand on the opposite shoulder, and together they pushed him back into his seat.

"Obviously, I didn't make myself clear enough," Jedidiah said his tone turning icy. "I'm not selling my land, not to Perkins, not to anyone. Your intimidation tactics won't work on me."

The first man leaned in, his face inches from Jedidiah's. "You're making a big mistake, Davenport. Perkins doesn't like to be refused."

Jedidiah met the man's gaze unflinchingly. "Then he'll have to learn to live with disappointment."

The second man tightened his grip on Jedidiah's shoulder, but before he could speak, Matthew Colton entered the restaurant, a western hat on his head and a gun strapped to his side. His eyes narrowed as he assessed the situation, flanked by the two armed men he had hired as guards.

"Everything alright here, Jed?" Matt asked, his presence causing the two men to loosen their grip. They both took a step backwards bumping into two men standing directly behind them. They were the two drivers that Matthew had mentioned earlier.

They had been sitting quietly at a table in the corner of the room. Each had been preparing to step in and defend their employer.

Jedidiah seized the opportunity, standing up swiftly. "I was just leaving," he declared, facing the two antagonists. "Tell Perkins this isn't the end. I'll fight him every step of the way."

The men backed off, but one of them sneered, "You'll regret it if you don't sign that paper, Davenport!"

As Jedidiah and Matthew left the restaurant, Jedidiah couldn't help but feel a surge of defiance mixed with unease. The encounter had only hardened Jedidiah's resolve, but he knew things were escalating.

"Perkins really means business doesn't he?" Colton asked as they stepped outside.

"We need to be prepared, Matt. That man will stop at nothing to get what he wants." Jedidiah replied, his mind already racing ahead.

As they walked back towards the freight office, Jedidiah couldn't shake the image of the airship from the newspaper. Maybe, just maybe, it was the key to outmaneuvering Perkins. As he mused over this new possibility, Jedidiah felt a flicker of hope amidst the looming threats. The fight was far from over, and he was ready for it.

When they reached the loaded wagon, Jedidiah saw his horse tied to the rear of it and next to it another horse brandishing familiar gear.

"Isn't that your horse?" Jedidiah Davenport turned to his childhood friend. "That's the saddle from the magazine you sent away for!"

"I'm going with you!" Matthew replied simply, as he placed his foot into the stirrup and mounted his horse.

"What about the freight office?" Jedidiah asked with a tone of concern.

"My assistant is more than capable of managing things while I'm away," Matthew Colton replied assuredly. "I've already left him with all the instructions he needs to run the place as needed."

Jedidiah simply laughed as he shook his head and mounted his stead. He knew that once his friend made up his mind to do something there was no changing it.

With Jedidiah and Matthew in the lead, the supply wagon and drivers in tow, and the two armed guards pulling up the rear, the group started down the dusty streets of Sheffield to begin their journey to Spoon Fork.

The trip was long and the air filled with a tense silence, each man lost in his thoughts. The sun began its descent, casting long shadows across the landscape. The rhythmic clop of the horses' hooves and the creaking of the wagon wheels were the only sounds breaking the silence.

Jedidiah couldn't help but glance occasionally at

Matt, grateful for his friend's unwavering support. Their friendship, forged in childhood and strengthened over the years, was a source of strength in these challenging times.

As they rode, Jedidiah's mind kept returning to the airship article. The more he thought about it, the more it seemed like a viable solution. An airship could revolutionize transportation, not just for his business, but for the entire region. It could be the edge he needed against Perkins' manipulative tactics.

Jedidiah turned to Matthew Colton, sharing his idea with him. He told him about the newspaper article and pointed towards his saddlebag where he had placed the paper in question.

"Oh yes!" Matthew replied enthusiastically. "I saw that article yesterday! It was amazing! I never thought it would be possible to travel all the way around the world!"

"That's just the marvels of modern science!" Jedidiah exclaimed, his face lighting up more than it had in a long time. "Just think of the possibilities! If I were to replace our wagons at each depot with an airship we could deliver our freight in a fraction of the time!"

"You think you could build one of those?" Matthew asked, genuinely curious.

Jedidiah chuckled as he reminded his friend that he had been quite an engineer before he took over his father's business. With a hint of pride in his voice, he asked, "Matt, have you forgotten the contraptions I've come up with over the years?"

Matthew's brow furrowed as he pretended not to recall. "You mean like..."

"Like the enhanced scope and range finder I built for my rifle," Jedidiah interjected, his eyes lighting up at the memory. "Remember that hunting trip two years back? How I could hit targets at distances we never thought possible?"

"Oh, right!" Matthew's face brightened with realization. "And wasn't there that... what did you call it... a mechanical calculator?"

"Exactly, the gear-driven mechanical calculator," Jedidiah said with a nod. "Helped us sort out the financial mess when we were expanding the business. Made calculations faster and reduced errors. You were quite impressed with that gadget."

Matthew laughed. "Impressed and confused by all those gears and levers."

"Hopefully you're still using the one I built for you to help balance the books in Sheffield."

"Wouldn't dream of using anything else!" Matthew laughed and then asked, "Didn't you also build something for the ranch? Some sort of water system?"

"Ah, yes, the wind-powered water pumps," Jedidiah replied, a touch of satisfaction in his tone.

"Revolutionized the way we managed water on the ranch. No more manual labor to draw water for the fields and livestock. It's all powered by the wind."

Matthew shook his head in admiration. "I have to admit, Jed, you've always had a knack for this sort of thing. Building an airship might not be too far-fetched for you after all."

Jedidiah's eyes sparkled with ambition. "Well, if I could tackle those projects, why not an airship? It might just be the solution we need to stay one step ahead of Perkins and his cronies."

The two friends continued talking as they rode. The journey back to Spoon Fork was mostly uneventful until they reached a point about halfway there. Jedidiah, leading the group, suddenly pulled on the reins, bringing his horse to a stop. Ahead of them, a wooden fence stretched across the path, a gate barring their way – a new addition to the landscape that Jedidiah had never seen before.

"Since when is there a fence or a gate here?" Jedidiah muttered, his eyes scanning the horizon for any signs of who might have put it up.

Matthew, riding alongside him, squinted at the fence. "I've never seen it before. It looks new."

The drivers and guards, following their lead, also came to a halt, exchanging confused glances.

"It wasn't here this morning when we came through, Mr. Davenport!" One of the two drivers commented with a look of confusion on his face.

"Since when is there a fence or a gate here?"

Everything became quiet for a moment as everyone tried to puzzle out what was going on. Suddenly the stillness was shattered by the sharp crack of gunfire as bullets began whizzing past their heads!

CHAPTER V

Unseen Boundaries

The sudden gunfire sent a jolt of adrenaline through the group. Jedidiah instinctively ducked, motioning for everyone to take cover. Amidst the chaos, he managed to scan the horizon, trying to locate the source of the shots.

"Stay down!" he shouted, his voice commanding amidst the panic. The sound of bullets whistling through the air was unnervingly close.

Matthew, quick to react, drew his revolver, his eyes darting around the landscape, trying to spot their assailants. "Who's shooting at us?" he called out, his voice edged with urgency.

The drivers and guards, experienced in their line of work, swiftly took defensive positions, their weapons at the ready. The horses, spooked by the sudden noise, whinnied and shuffled nervously.

Despite their predicament, Jedidiah suddenly looked at his friend with a nostalgic smile on his face. "You remember that time we got caught in the storm up by Miller's Ridge?"

Matt laughed heartily. "How could I forget? You were convinced we were going to be struck by lightning, but I was more worried about losing our hats to the wind."

"That was the day I realized you had a knack for keeping your cool in tough situations," Jedidiah remarked. "Seems like you haven't changed a bit."

A gruff voice called out from a concealed position behind the fence. "This land's been claimed! You're trespassing!"

Jedidiah's eyes narrowed as he tried to peer through the brush where the voice seemed to come from. "Claimed by who? This is a public thoroughfare!"

"Not anymore!" the voice retorted, followed by another volley of warning shots.

Matthew, still aiming his revolver towards the fence, whispered to Jedidiah, "This has to be Perkins' doing."

Jedidiah nodded in agreement, his mind racing for a solution. "We need to defuse this without bloodshed."

One of the guards, a seasoned veteran, whispered back, "We can try to flank them, create a distraction."

Jedidiah considered the suggestion, weighing their options. "No, let's not escalate this. We talk first. If that fails, we'll find another way around."

Taking a deep breath, Jedidiah called out, "We mean no harm! We just need to pass through. Let's talk this out!"

There was a tense moment of silence, then the voice replied, "Turn back now, or the next shots won't be for show!"

Matthew glanced at Jedidiah, "Looks like talking isn't working."

Jedidiah, thinking quickly, shouted, "We're not looking for trouble, but we won't be bullied either. We have right of way here!"

The tense standoff continued, with Jedidiah and his group cautiously waiting for the next move. The sun was inching its way down the horizon, casting long shadows over the dusty road.

Suddenly, a figure emerged from behind the fence, accompanied by five armed men. Among them, three were recognizable from Spoon Fork, while the other two were from the Cobblestone Inn.

"Leroy Johnson," Jedidiah muttered under his breath, recognizing the face of the man in front.

"Well, well, Davenport," Leroy called out, a smug tone in his voice. "Seems like you've run into a bit of trouble."

"What's the meaning of this, Johnson?" Jedidiah demanded, tightening the grip on his rifle.

Leroy waved a paper in the air. "This land now belongs to Perkins, and you're trespassing."

Jedidiah's eyes flashed with anger. "Blocking a public road like this is illegal."

"This ain't a public road no more!" Leroy chuckled. "Besides, Perkins dictates the law around here. And he says this road's closed to you."

There was a moment of tense silence as Jedidiah assessed the situation. Finally, he nodded at his men. "Turn the wagon around. We're heading back to Sheffield."

Matthew whispered to Jedidiah, "What's our next move?"

Jedidiah's gaze remained fixed on Leroy and his men. "You and I are gonna find another way to Spoon Fork."

As they began to turn the wagon around, Leroy called out, "Remember, Davenport, Perkins doesn't like to be crossed. This is just a taste of what's to come!"

Jedidiah ignored the threat, focusing on getting his men out of the situation safely. The next few minutes were filled with a heavy silence, each man lost in his thoughts about the escalating conflict.

A short distance down the road, Jedidiah and Matthew began discussing plans for an alternative route to Spoon Fork. "This isn't over," Jedidiah said, his voice determined. "Perkins has pushed me too far this time."

Matthew nodded in agreement. "We'll find another way around. He can't control every path to

Spoon Fork."

Jedidiah and Matthew stayed with the others until they reached a fork in the road. It was here that they parted company with the four men.

As night fell, Jedidiah and his friend Matthew made a brief stop allowing the horses to drink from a small creek.

Back on the road, under a starlit sky, Jedidiah felt a renewed sense of purpose. He was more determined than ever not to give in to Elijah Perkins or the railroad.

As they approached the outskirts of Spoon Fork, Jedidiah felt a surge of confidence. Perkins might have wealth and influence, but Jedidiah had something far more powerful. He had innovation and the resolve to see it through.

Arriving in town, they headed straight to the Davenport Dispatch & Delivery headquarters. The building, though still bearing some scars from the recent explosion, stood resiliently, symbolizing Jedidiah's determination to overcome adversity. Jim Davis and his men had repaired most of the damage caused by the explosion. They hadn't had a chance to paint yet, but at least the building looked whole and intact

Considering the toll the day's events had taken on him, Jedidiah decided it would be better to stay in town rather than continue riding to his ranch. He chose to rent a room at the hotel for some much-

Under a starlit sky, Jedidiah felt
a renewed sense of purpose.

needed rest before facing the challenges of a new day.

"This way we can go to the land office as soon as they open in the morning." He explained to Matthew.

"Good idea!" Matthew exclaimed. "However I should probably go rent the room just in case they don't want you staying here!"

Jedidiah took a deep breath and sighed. "You're probably right…" He admitted. "I'll put our horses and saddles up while you're taking care of that."

Matthew didn't waste any time in renting a room with two beds, hoping the hotel manager wouldn't inquire about the second occupant. After noticing the manager heading to a back room, Matthew gestured for Jedidiah to enter. They promptly went upstairs and settled into their room.

In the quiet of the night, with the town asleep, Jedidiah lay in bed, his mind racing with plans for the airship. He envisioned a future where his business soared above the limitations of land and rail, free from Perkins' grasp.

****

The next morning greeted Jedidiah and Matthew with a clear, blue sky. Spoon Fork was just waking up, the streets slowly coming to life with the hustle of early risers. Despite the lingering fatigue from the previous day's events, Jedidiah felt a sense of urgency. He and Matthew quickly readied themselves, their first stop being the land office to investigate the validity of the deed Leroy Johnson had flaunted.

They walked through the quiet streets, the tension from yesterday's incident still heavy in the air. As they approached the land office, Jedidiah's mind was a whirlwind of thoughts. If the deed was legitimate, it meant a significant complication in his ongoing struggle against Perkins. However, Jedidiah clung to a sliver of hope that it was just another one of Perkins' bluffs.

The land office was a small, unassuming building, but it held the answers to many of the town's disputes and claims. The clerk, a bespectacled man with a meticulous nature, greeted them as they entered. "Morning, gentlemen. How can I assist you today?"

"We're here to inquire about a recent land claim," Jedidiah stated, getting straight to the point. He described the location of the land and the encounter with Leroy Johnson.

The clerk's brows furrowed as he sifted through his records. After a moment, he located the file and pulled out a document. "Yes, there was a recent claim filed for that land. It appears to be in order and legally binding," he said, handing the deed to

Jedidiah.

Matthew leaned over to examine the deed alongside His friend. The document looked official, complete with the necessary stamps and signatures. Jedidiah's heart sank as he realized the depth of Perkins' reach.

"Is there anything that can be done to dispute this claim?" Matthew asked, his voice tinged with frustration.

The clerk shook his head. "Not unless you can prove it was obtained under false pretenses or by force. Do you have any evidence to suggest that?"

Jedidiah pondered for a moment, then replied, "Not at the moment, but we will look into it. Thank you for your help."

The two young men were about to leave when an idea suddenly struck Davenport. He turned around on his heel and reproached the clerk's desk. "Do you by any chance have a map of the whole valley showing the proposed route for the railroad?"

The clerk, slightly taken aback by the sudden request, nodded. "Yes, we do have a map detailing the proposed railway plans. It's a public record." He walked over to a large cabinet and pulled out a rolled-up parchment. Unfurling it on the desk, he revealed a detailed map of the valley, with the proposed railroad line marked in red.

Jedidiah and Matthew leaned over the map,

studying it intently. The line snaked through the valley, then took a wild turn straight through the middle of the Davenport ranch.

"It goes nowhere near the land he put the fence and gate on!" Jedidiah exclaimed. "That proves he purchased it just to hold up my business and try to force me to sell!"

"I wonder why he chose such a wild path for the railroad…" Matthew casually remarked as he studied the map intently.

A look of confusion came over Jedidiah's face and he asked, "What do you mean?"

Matthew pointed to two locations on the map. "Here and here, he's deliberately deviating the track, diverting it through your property!"

Jedidiah's eyes narrowed as he studied the map. "You're right! This land over here is more of a straight shot between those two points. It's flatter and would save the railroad a lot of time."

Matthew looked up, meeting Jedidiah's determined gaze. "Perkins is intentionally targeting your ranch!"

"But why?" Jedidiah gasped. "He must have some reason behind it!"

Matthew quickly agreed and said, "I bet you, if we try hard enough, we can find out what it is!"

Jedidiah nodded, his mind already racing with possibilities. "We'll need to act fast. Perkins is not going to slow down his efforts."

After another moment of studying the map, Jedidiah rolled it up and handed it back to the clerk. Thanking him, they stepped out of the land office, the weight of their discovery heavy on their minds.

The streets of Spoon Fork were gradually coming alive with the morning bustle. Jedidiah and Matthew navigated through the crowd, deep in conversation about their next steps. They discussed reaching out to the owner of that parcel to see if they had been contacted by anyone from the railroad. They needed every possible angle to uncover Perkins' plans.

As they walked along, Jedidiah's resolve strengthened. Despite the daunting battle ahead, he was not alone. Engrossed in their conversation, they were interrupted by a familiar voice calling out, "Jed, a moment, please."

Jedidiah turned to see Sheriff Thompson approaching, his expression serious. "Sheriff, what can I do for you?"

"I need to speak with you privately in my office," Sheriff Thompson said, his tone indicating the urgency of the matter.

Matthew nodded at Jedidiah, understanding the need for discretion. "I'll head to the freight office and ready the horses," he said before departing.

Jedidiah followed Sheriff Thompson to the small, modest building serving as the sheriff's office. Inside, the sheriff motioned for Jedidiah to sit.

As the two men began to engage in a serious conversation, Matthew made his way to the main branch of Davenport Dispatch & Delivery. The streets of Spoon Fork were now bustling with activity, but the weight of recent events hung in the air like a dense fog.

Upon arriving at the freight office, Matthew was greeted by Mr. Clayton, the manager and dispatcher of the Spoon Fork branch. Mr. Clayton, a seasoned man with a keen eye for logistics, had been running the day-to-day operations efficiently.

"Matthew, good to see you," Mr. Clayton said, looking a bit puzzled. "What are you doing in Spoon Fork? Shouldn't you be running the Sheffield office for Jedidiah?"

"I'm actually here to help him out with the trouble he's been having with the railroad." Matthew Colton explained. "You've probably noticed by now that your wagon never made it back from Sheffield last night."

Mr. Clayton's countenance suddenly changed to a bit of nervousness. "Oh yes! I did notice that! I was actually getting ready to go telegraph your office to find out what happened. We have freight that needs to go out you know!"

Matthew sat down on the edge of Mr. Clayton's desk and said, "Unfortunately, the line between Spoon Fork and Sheffield may be shut down for a while."

"What!" Clayton exclaimed. "What's happened?"

"Elijah Perkins purchased a piece of land that we've been using for a road. He's put up a fence and has Johnson with five armed men guarding the gate.

"This is very serious indeed!" Mr. Clayton suddenly looked exasperated. "Where's Jed? He's still in town isn't he?"

"Yes, he is, but he's caught up with Sheriff Thompson at the moment," Matthew replied, his tone conveying the urgency of their situation. "Is there anything I can do to help while I'm here?"

"As a matter of fact..." Mr. Clayton glanced around the room as if he was trying to find some kind of project he could get Matthew to work on. "You can help me with this!"

Together, the two of them began reviewing the dispatch schedule, ensuring that all deliveries were properly organized. Their focus was on maintaining safe and efficient routes amidst the town's growing tensions. Matthew's keen attention to detail brought a sense of control and reassurance to the process.

Mr. Clayton shared the latest updates from their drivers and reported on the condition of the roads. "We'll have to be on the lookout for other blockades," he informed Matthew. "The situation's getting trickier by the day."

Matthew nodded, his mind processing the information. "Keep an eye out for any unusual activity. We can't afford any more setbacks," he advised.

After finishing up at the office, Matthew headed to the stables to ready their horses. The stable, a familiar and comforting place for Matthew, was a stark contrast to the tension that filled the town. He methodically prepared the horses, double-checking their saddles and bridles. The rhythmic sounds of the stable allowed him a moment of quiet reflection, a brief respite from the whirlwind of events.

With the horses ready and waiting, Matthew lingered for a moment, gazing out towards the main street of Spoon Fork. He knew that whatever Jedidiah and Sheriff Thompson were discussing it had to be important.

"Jedidiah, I won't beat around the bush any longer," Sheriff Thompson began, his face grave. "We've found something in the debris from the explosion at your office. Something that could change the course of our investigation."

Jedidiah leaned forward, his interest piqued. "What did you find?"

The sheriff retrieved a small object from a drawer and handed it to Jedidiah. It was an intricately designed pocket watch. Davenport's heart skipped a beat as he realized it belonged to his trusted foreman, Jim Davis!

CHAPTER VI

Betrayals and Secret Deals

"Are you positive?" the Sheriff asked reluctantly.

"This is definitely Jim's watch! I gave it to him last year for his birthday," Jedidiah replied.

Sheriff Thompson nodded. "That's what I was afraid of," he said. He momentarily took the object back, opened it up, and pointed inside the lid. "I really didn't need you to identify it. This inscription did that for me..."

'To Jim Davis,

In gratitude for years of steadfast loyalty and true friendship.

Your dedication is unmatched.

Jedidiah, 1880'

Davenport's mind raced. The implications were

Sheriff Thompson momentarily took
the watch back and opened the lid.

serious, but he couldn't jump to conclusions. "Sheriff, I know Jim. He wouldn't sabotage my business. There's got to be another explanation."

"I hope you're right, Jed, but we can't ignore this evidence. We both know he was in town around the time of the explosion," Sheriff Thompson stated, his expression growing more serious. "You even seemed surprised that he was here and not out protecting your ranch."

Jedidiah sighed, his mind drifting back to the day he first encountered Jim Davis—the day that had forged their bond. "Did I ever tell you how I met Jim?"

"No you never did," the Sheriff shook his head.

"About five years ago," Jedidiah began, his voice distant as he recalled the event. "I was just starting to build up my ranch, and things were... tough, to say the least. One evening, I was out with my small herd when a bunch of rustlers came riding up."

The memory was so vivid in Jedidiah's mind; he could still hear the sounds of the gunshots and the chaos around him. He remembered it all as he said, "I grabbed my rifle and tried to hold them off, but I was outnumbered. They were experienced, and it was clear I was losing ground. Then, out of nowhere, Jim rode in. He was like a force of nature with his six-shooter."

Jedidiah's voice grew somber. "I took a bullet to

the shoulder. Without Jim, I wouldn't have stood a chance. He not only helped me fend them off, but he also tended to my wound, dug the bullet out, and bandaged me up. He saved my life and my ranch that day."

Sheriff Thompson listened intently, the gravity of the story not lost on him. "Sounds like you owe him a lot."

"I do," Jedidiah agreed, his voice filled with a mix of gratitude and concern. "That's why I can't believe he'd be involved in anything that would harm me or my business. Jim's been more than a ranch hand; he's been a loyal friend."

Sheriff Thompson nodded, understanding the depth of their relationship. "We'll have to investigate further, Jed. For now, keep an eye on things. Let me know if you remember anything else that might help."

Jedidiah clenched the watch in his hand, feeling the weight of the situation. "I understand, Sheriff. I'll talk to Jim. Maybe there's an innocent explanation."

The sheriff gave Jedidiah a nod of understanding. "Keep me informed, Jed. We need to get to the bottom of this."

Jedidiah left the sheriff's office with the pocket watch in his hand and a heavy heart. As he walked towards the freight office, he knew he had to confront Jim. The truth had to come out, no matter what.

As he approached the freight office, he saw Matthew waiting with the horses. Jedidiah explained the situation, and together they prepared to leave for the ranch. The ride back would be long, filled with apprehension and uncertainty.

The two men mounted their horses and rode out of town. After riding for about ten minutes, Jedidiah pulled his horse's reins short, causing it to come to a stop. Matthew, seeing this, did the same.

"What's going on?" Colton asked confused. "Why are we stopping?"

"I've changed my mind, Matt. I can wait to confront Jim." Jedidiah's expression showed that his decision was firm. "Let's ride out to that land we spotted on the map and talk to the owner. I happen to know right where the shack he lives in is located."

Matthew looked at Jedidiah, noting the determination in his friend's eyes. "Alright, anything you say. You just lead the way."

The two men steered their horses in a new direction, heading towards the remote property. The ride was quiet, each man lost in his thoughts about the situation unfolding around them. The landscape gradually changed as they moved away from Spoon Fork, becoming increasingly rugged and isolated.

After a considerable ride, the outline of a small cabin appeared on the horizon, nestled in a secluded part of the valley. As they drew closer, Jedidiah's eyes narrowed, scanning the surroundings for any sign of trouble. The area seemed deserted, with only the sounds of nature filling the air.

They dismounted near the shack, their horses breathing heavily from the journey. Jedidiah approached the door cautiously, leaving his rifle tied to his saddle, while Matthew, with his pistol attached to his side, was prepared to draw it at a moment's notice. He knocked firmly.

After a moment of silence, the door creaked open, revealing an elderly man with a weathered face and cautious eyes. He looked at Jedidiah and Matthew warily.

"Can I help you gentlemen?" the old man asked, his voice rough from years of living in the harsh wilderness.

"We hope so," Jedidiah replied, introducing himself and Matthew. "We're here to talk about your land. Specifically, about any recent contact you might have had with the railroad or anyone associated with Elijah Perkins."

The man's expression changed slightly, a hint of apprehension flickering in his eyes. "I don't know what you're talking about," he said, but there was a tremor in his voice that suggested otherwise.

Jedidiah pressed on, explaining their findings from the map and their suspicions about Perkins' intentions. As he spoke, the man continued to act defensive and nervous. Jedidiah asked if they could come in and the owner reluctantly agreed.

Once inside the modest shack, the old man, introducing himself as George Buchanan, continued denying any contact with Perkins or any other representative of the railroad.

"What about a man named Johnson?" Matthew spoke up. "He's Perkins' number one hired gun."

"What's the matter, are you deaf?" the elderly man, replied with growing anger. "I told you ain't nobody been here offering me no money for my land!"

Jedidiah with a more calm voice of reason said, "Mr. George..."

"Buchanan!"

"Mr. Buchanan," Jedidiah continued, "I would like to make you an offer. I would like to buy your land."

"Buy my land?" The elderly man's eyes widened in surprise. "Why would you want to do a fool thing like that? My land is worthless!"

"I'll be honest with you, Mr. Buchanan..."

"George!"

"What?"

"Just call me George!"

"George, I'll be honest with you," Jedidiah continued again, "I want to offer this land to the railroad as an alternative to running their track down the middle of my ranch."

"It would benefit everyone concerned!" Matthew excitedly spoke up. "It would be a more direct path for the railroad and Jedidiah wouldn't have to split his grazing land in half."

"Plus, I would see to it that you received a considerable profit for selling it to me," Jedidiah Davenport quickly added.

"It's ain't for sale!" the old man suddenly blurted out.

Jedidiah looked confused for a moment and then said, "But you haven't even let me make you an offer yet..."

"It's ain't for sale at any price!"

"But Mr. Buchanan... I mean, George, you could move into town and live comfortably the rest of your life on what I plan to offer you!"

"Maybe I like living secluded, from the rest of the world, in the middle of nowhere!"

This back and forth went on for a few more minutes before the old man finally got frustrated enough to blurt out, "It ain't for sale because I've already sold it!"

"Come again..." Jedidiah and Matthew were both suddenly taken off guard by this comment.

Still visibly frustrated, the elderly man said, "I sold it weeks ago to Perkins! I signed the deed over to him and gave him a bill of sale. He asked me to keep living here until he told me otherwise, and if anyone came snooping around, I was to deny everything!"

Jedidiah and Matthew exchanged looks of shock and disbelief.

"Weeks ago?" Jedidiah asked perplexed. "The whole time they've been trying to force me to sell my land, the railroad has had the means to a more viable option in the palms of their hands!"

"But why haven't they registered the deed at the land office?" Matthew asked, equally confused. "It's showing that it's still registered to the original owner." He looked directly at Mr. Buchanan as he said that last part.

"It's the truth!" The elderly man rushed across the room to his fireplace and grabbed a cigar box off the mantle. He pulled out his copy of the bill of sale and showed it to his guests. It was written out to the D.&R.W. Railroad.

Jedidiah's nostrils began to flare as the realization of what had been going on settled in. "They definitely have some type of ulterior motive for wanting my land and that's something we need to figure out!"

"Please don't let Mr. Perkins or his henchman Mr. Johnson know I told you about any of this!" Mr. Buchanan pleaded with the young ranch owner.

"Don't worry about anything, George. Just don't tell anyone you saw us here today!" He thanked the elderly man for his honesty and assured him that they would do everything in their power to protect him from Perkins.

Riding back to Spoon Fork, Jedidiah and Matthew discussed their next steps. They realized they needed to gather more evidence and inform the Sheriff of their discovery. The fight was far from over, but they were determined to stand their ground.

Upon reaching town, Jedidiah Davenport and Matthew Colton headed straight for Sheriff Thompson's office, the weight of their discovery pressing heavily on their minds.

Sheriff Thompson looked up in surprise as the two men entered his office, their faces etched with urgency. "Jed, Matt, what brings you back so soon?" he inquired, sensing something significant.

"Sheriff, we've got new information about the railroad situation," Jedidiah began, his voice steady but laden with concern. "It's about the land deal with Perkins."

Sheriff Thompson leaned forward, his interest piqued. "Go on."

Jedidiah recounted their visit to George Buchanan's shack, describing the elderly man's initial reluctance and the eventual revelation. "Mr. Buchanan sold his land to Perkins weeks ago, Sheriff. The deed's been signed over but was never registered at the land office. Perkins has been holding it back for some reason."

Matthew chimed in, "That land is better suited for the railroad than Jed's. It's a straighter path, less disruptive. But Perkins has been fixated on forcing Jed to sell."

The sheriff's brows furrowed as he processed this information. "That doesn't make any sense. Why would Perkins pressure you to sell if he already has a more suitable option?"

"Exactly," Jedidiah said. "This is just more proof that Perkins' interest in my property goes beyond the obvious. There's something we're not seeing yet."

Sheriff Thompson stood up, his expression turning serious. "This changes things. We need to find out what Perkins is after. And why he's keeping this land deal a secret."

"I agree," Jedidiah said firmly. "There's a piece of this puzzle we're missing, and it's time we found it."

The sheriff nodded. "I'll look into the legal aspects of this unregistered deed. Meanwhile, Jed, keep your eyes open and be careful. If Perkins finds out we're onto him, there's no telling what he might do."

Jedidiah and Matthew acknowledged the sheriff's advice with a nod, realizing the gravity of the situation. As they left the office, the sun was just beginning to set over the horizon. The revelation about the land deal cast a new light on the conflict, and both men knew that the coming days would bring challenges they had yet to imagine.

After remounting their horses, they rode off once again toward the Davenport Ranch. By the time they finally reached there, the sun had completely set. However, the moon was big and bright in the sky, providing enough light for them to see.

The two men wasted no time bedding down their horses in Jedidiah's stable before retiring to his elaborate Victorian-style home—a touch of elegance in the Wild West.

They were immediately greeted by Jedidiah's loyal and faithful servants, Agatha Porter and Pat Bennington.

"Well, it's about time you came home!" Agatha exclaimed in a scolding tone. "We were beginning to worry those men from the railroad had done you in!"

"Don't you listen to her, Jed!" Pat laughed. "She's had her friends over all day yesterday and today playing pinochle and eating ladyfinger sandwiches!"

"We did no such thing!" Agatha protested. "I mean I did no such thing!"

"You didn't?" Pat laughed. "Then who did I make all those sandwiches for?"

The older woman reached up and adjusted the

bun on top of her head. "I may have a couple of the gals over but we weren't playing pinochle... not the whole time anyway..."

"Poker?" Pat winked at Jedidiah and Matthew.

"Bridge!" Agatha Porter was furious as she glared at the little, round-bellied, bearded man in front of her. "And you know very well you ate most of those sandwiches yourself!"

By now, Jedidiah and Matthew had both burst out laughing. "It's fine, I don't care," Jedidiah remarked as he motioned towards Matthew Colton. "Aggie, Pat, you both remember my friend Matt."

"Why, Mr. Colton!" Agatha's eyes lit up at the sight of the young man standing next to Jedidiah. "I didn't even notice you there!"

"Well maybe if you'd stop flapping your gums long enough you might be able to pay attention more!" Pat playfully taunted the older woman.

"I'll get you for that!" She replied then turned her direction back to Jedidiah and Matthew. "What brings you out here, Matt?"

"He's come to help me with Perkins, Johnson, and the rest of the railroad," Jedidiah explained. Glancing upstairs, he asked, "Do you mind preparing the room next to mine for Matthew to stay in?"

"Preparing?" Agatha asked confused.

"Yeah, you know fresh clean linen and... I don't know whatever else needs to be done to prepare a room for a guest..."

The older woman audibly gasped and asked, "Jedidiah Davenport, are you insinuating that I don't keep a clean house?"

"No... I just meant..."

"Never mind what you meant!" she exclaimed, turning on her heel to walk away. "I'll just go upstairs and change the sheets and spread because, apparently, I spend all day jumping up and down on the beds with my shoes on! While I'm at it, I'll get the chickens out of the dresser drawers and might as well get the pigs out of there too. You know how I like to keep livestock in the spare rooms!"

"She's just joking, Matt," Jedidiah said, glancing nervously at his friend. "She just feels like I insulted her in front of you." He quickly turned to Pat for confirmation, asking, "Isn't that right?"

"Absolutely!" Pat nodded his head. "Everybody knows I keep the chickens and the pigs in the kitchen. It's more convenient!" As he said this, he turned on his heel and headed off. "I'll go finish cooking. I'm sure both of you are starving!"

"Matt, they're both joking!" Jedidiah was afraid his friend might believe what his servants were saying.

Matthew Colton laughed and shook his head. "It's okay, Jed. This isn't my first time meeting them."

Davenport took a sigh of relief and said, "You're

gonna love the improvements I've made around here since your last visit. You'll now have your own private bath with heated water!"

"Heated water?" Matthew asked, confused.

"Follow me!" Jedidiah motioned for his friend to step outside with him. He led him around back to the windmill-powered water pump they had discussed earlier. He pointed to a large storage unit on legs. "That holds all of the cold water." He explained.

"How do you heat it?" Matthew asked curiously.

"Follow me..." Jedidiah opened a door on what appeared to be a brick tower attached to the house. They ascended the stairs to the top. "This tank inside holds the water to be heated. It's just below the level of the water tower outside. I have a line connected to it that allows gravity to take its course."

Matthew stood in awe as he watched Jedidiah place precut wood under the metal container, adding it to the already burning fire.

"I have lines connected from this tank to the kitchen and all the private baths in the house."

Matthew was impressed with his friend's creative ingenuity. "If you're smart enough to think of stuff like this, I don't think you'll have any problem outsmarting Elijah Perkins and his men!"

"I hope you're right!" Jedidiah replied as he

turned to lead the way back down.

After descending the stairs and stepping outside, Jedidiah and Matthew were caught off guard by a sudden commotion at the front of the house. As they rounded the corner, a horse galloped wildly toward them. The rider, barely clinging on, was someone Jedidiah recognized as one of his own ranch hands. His face was taut with urgency.

The horse came to a sudden, jarring stop, hooves digging into the earth, stirring up a cloud of dust around them. The ranch hand gasped for air, his eyes wide with alarm. "Mr. Davenport!" he exclaimed, his voice trembling with a mix of fear and haste. "Something's happened!"

Jedidiah's heart sank as he braced himself for the worst. "What is it? Speak up, man!" he demanded, his voice steady despite the dread that clawed at his chest.

The ranch hand leaned forward, his words spilling out in a frantic rush. "It's... it's..." But before he could finish, a sharp crack echoed across the field, silencing his next words. Jedidiah's eyes narrowed as he turned toward the sound, his mind racing. In the distance, black smoke began to rise!

CHAPTER VII

Blueprints of Defiance

The night air at the Davenport Ranch was split by the urgent cries of the ranch hands and the ominous cloud of smoke from the distant fire. Jedidiah and Matthew wasted no time saddling fresh horses and following the ranch hand across the vast field.

After a short ride, they were greeted by a towering inferno billowing from one of Jedidiah's enormous hay barns. This storage shed, a titan among farm structures, dwarfed the surrounding buildings. Its cavernous interior was capable of storing an immense quantity of hay.

Jedidiah's heart sank at the sight. Fortunately, the barn itself wasn't ablaze yet, but the hay inside was a roaring furnace. He knew the fire threatened not just the barn but the entire ranch if it spread. Springing into action, he shouted orders, his voice cutting through the chaos.

"Get to the tower, now!" Jedidiah urged the workers toward the huge water tower, filled by some of his other windmill-powered pumps. This was different from the one he used to supply water for his house. This silent guardian usually provided hydration for the fields but was now their main line of defense against the encroaching flames. "We need every bit of water we can get."

Matthew, understanding the urgency, rallied the men, organizing a human chain from the pond to the barn. The air was thick with smoke, and the heat from the fire was intense, but they worked with a singular focus, passing buckets of water along the line.

Meanwhile, Jedidiah, with a group of men, maneuvered the large horse-drawn water carts from the tower to the barn. The carts, usually used for irrigating fields, were quickly repurposed to fight the fire. Men climbed atop the barn, using the water from the carts to douse the flames, while others on the ground fought to keep the fire contained within the barn's thick wooden walls.

As they battled the flames, they were overshadowed by the barn's magnitude. Its usually imposing size, was now a daunting challenge as they struggled to reach the upper sections where the fire reached. The structure, built to store enough hay to feed their livestock through the harshest of winters, now threatened to become a colossal pyre.

Jedidiah, Matthew, and the ranch hands worked tirelessly into the night, their faces illuminated by the fire's glow. It was a grueling battle, but their determination was unwavering. Gradually, the flames began to diminish, beaten back by the relentless efforts of the men.

As the fire was finally brought under control, the realization dawned on Jedidiah. This was no accident. The fire had started too quickly, too fiercely. It was a deliberate act, a message sent through flames.

Exhausted, covered in soot and sweat, Jedidiah stood before the smoldering remains of the hay, his mind racing. This attack on his livelihood was a clear escalation of the conflict surrounding his land and the railroad. The question now was: what about his land made anyone willing to resort to such destructive measures to acquire it?

After instructing his men to return to the bunkhouse and rest, Jedidiah turned to Matthew, proposing they do the same at his house.

"It's too bad they don't have private baths in the bunkhouse like you," Matthew remarked sympathetically. "I'm sure they could use a good freshening up."

Jedidiah laughed and said, "Don't worry, they're set up just fine." As he mounted his horse, he added, "They have their own windmill, water tower, and heated storage tank, along with more than half a dozen private shower stalls to freshen up in."

"You think of everything, don't you?" Matthew Colton laughed as he mounted his horse.

Just as they were about to ride back to Davenport's house, another man on horseback came galloping up. It was the foreman, Jim Davis.

Jedidiah's long-time and trusted friend was clearly out of breath as he said, "Jed, I came as fast as I could, but I was patrolling the fence line on the north end of the ranch!"

"If you were that far out how did you know about the fire?" Matthew asked, almost accusingly.

"I saw the smoke!" Jim replied, defensively. "It's a good thing it's a clear night with a full moon or I'd have never spotted it!"

"Well, it's out now and that's the most important thing," Jedidiah remarked as he took a deep breath. "There was some roof damage a few timbers here and there but nothing that can't be repaired."

"All of the hay you had stored in there is gone!" Matthew quickly added.

"It's okay I think I have other plans for that building now anyway," Jedidiah added with an air of mystery.

"I wish I could have been here to help put it out!" the ranch foreman added with a tone of regret.

"Don't worry about it, Jim," Jedidiah replied as

he turned his horse in the direction of his house. "Don't go too far in the morning I want to talk to you about something."

With that being said, Jedidiah and Matthew rode back to the house. Jedidiah showed Matthew how to operate the controls to fill the tub with both hot and cold water. After this, he retreated to his own room and bathtub, where he soaked for what felt like hours. Once they had each enjoyed a hearty meal downstairs in the kitchen, the two men retired to their rooms.

****

The next morning, Jedidiah sought out Jim Davis. He found him in the stables, busy tending to the horses. Their conversation was fraught with difficulty as Jedidiah showed Jim the watch, seeking an explanation. Jim, looking bewildered, insisted that he had lost the watch days before the explosion and swore that he had nothing to do with the sabotage.

The conversation left Jedidiah more confused than ever. He trusted Jim, but the evidence was hard to ignore. He decided to keep a close eye on the situation while continuing to investigate other leads.

Before returning to his house, Jedidiah gave Jim

Davis crudely drawn blueprints he had designed early that morning for the barn, featuring a retractable roof with large, hinged panels. These panels could be operated by a system of pulleys, gears, and cranks.

****

That evening, as Jedidiah and Matthew sat on the porch of Jedidiah's house, they discussed their next steps. The airship project was now crucial, serving not only as a business venture but also as a symbol of defiance against those seeking control.

"We'll start construction first thing Monday morning," Jedidiah declared, a determined glint in his eye. "Perkins may have control of the roadways, but he can't control the skies."

Matthew nodded in agreement, adding, "And I'll keep digging into Perkins' motives for the railroad path. There's more to this than just wanting your land."

The reality of building an airship suddenly dawned on Matthew Colton, who hadn't fully considered the task's enormity until now. "Monday is only two days away!" he exclaimed. "Have you even started planning how to build it?"

"No, but I think I know someone who can help," Jedidiah said, holding up the newspaper with the article about the man who had traveled around the world by airship. "It says here that Phineas B. Hargroves will be in Wichita all weekend for a convention to show off his creation."

"Wichita!" Matthew exclaimed. "That's quite a distance!"

"That's why we'll leave first thing in the morning and we should be there tomorrow night."

Matthew just shook his head and laughed. "Whatever you say, you're the boss!"

As they retired for the night, Jedidiah's last thoughts were of the airship, soaring high above the trials and tribulations of the land below. It was a dream that was quickly becoming a necessity, and he was ready to make it a reality.

****

Saturday morning found the two men up before anyone else on the ranch. They made themselves a hearty breakfast and were back on the road again before anyone even knew they were gone.

After spending the entirety of the day riding in the saddle, Jedidiah Davenport and Matthew Colton finally arrived in Wichita. As they entered the bustling city, they were immediately struck by its energy. "This place feels like a different world," Matthew remarked, taking in the sights and sounds of the city.

Jedidiah nodded in agreement. "It's the heartbeat of progress. This city makes our small towns look like they're standing still."

Suddenly, the hotel hosting the convention caught their eye. Above the building, the airship floated gracefully, a marvelous blend of engineering and imagination. It appeared to be tethered securely to the roof. A rope ladder dangled from its side, swaying gently in the breeze.

"That must be how Phineas got down!" Jedidiah remarked, referencing the ladder. "I bet there's a door on the roof going into the hotel."

"I bet you're right!" Matthew replied. "Otherwise he'd have quite a jump from the top of that building!"

After a brief chuckle, they spurred their horses towards a boarding stable at the end of the street. Once arrangements were made, they walked back to the hotel. Jedidiah decided to leave his rifle with their gear, while Matthew continued to wear his six-gun at his side.

The lobby of the hotel was teeming with people, a hub of excitement and innovation. They navigated through the crowd to the front desk, only to find out that all rooms were fully booked.

"What do we do now?" Matthew asked disappointed. "Should we find a place outside of town to camp out?

Above the building, the airship floated gracefully.

"Don't be so fast to throw in the towel," Jedidiah remarked as began to scan the crowd. He spotted a well-dressed man who seemed disinterested in the convention. "Hold on, Matt. Let me try something."

Jedidiah approached the man and said, "Excuse me, sir, I couldn't help but notice you seem a bit overwhelmed by all this commotion," he added with a grand gesture of his hand.

The man, wearing a weary expression, replied, "To be honest, I am. I came for a quiet stay, not for this circus."

Jedidiah seized the opportunity. "What if I could offer you a solution? We need a room, and you need peace and quiet."

After a brief negotiation, Jedidiah managed to secure the man's suite for them, albeit at a steep price.

"Never underestimate the power of persuasion and the right amount of cash," Jedidiah quipped as he returned to Matthew, showing off the key.

"How much did you have to give him for that?" Matthew Colton was almost afraid to find out the answer.

Jedidiah sighed and then chuckled. "Probably cost more than the entire top floor, but I don't care!" he declared, turning on his heel towards the dining room. "Let's eat. I'm starved!"

The dining room was filled with the clinking of

cutlery and the hum of lively conversations. They found a table near the back and settled in for an elegant meal.

Even though the airship itself was not visible from inside the building, there was a giant enlarged photo of the newspaper article attached to the wall across from them. It served as a constant reminder of why they were there.

As they ate, they couldn't help but eavesdrop on the conversations around them, picking up snippets about business deals being struck and the latest in technological innovation. It was clear that they were in the midst of a pivotal moment in history, and they were right at the heart of it.

"You know no matter what the reason for bringing us here, I'm glad we came!" Jedidiah glanced around the room and began to feel right at home amongst the inventors and engineers. "This is inspiring me to start back working on my own projects."

Jedidiah's gaze wandered across the dining room, eventually resting on a familiar figure at a distant table. He was in deep conversation with a young man whose features spoke of European origins.

"What made you stop?" Matthew asked curiously. "With your talent, you could be like that guy who invented the light bulb a couple of years ago... What was his name?

"Edison!" Jedidiah exclaimed excitedly. "Thomas Edison!"

"Yeah, that's the one!" Matthew replied.

"Matt, look over there," Jedidiah nudged his friend, pointing subtly. "That's Thomas Edison sitting over there!"

Matthew casually turned his head and looked in the direction Jedidiah indicated. "What's he doing here?" He asked, excitedly.

"He must be attending the convention. I can't miss this chance to meet him!" Jedidiah's eyes sparkled with excitement. Standing up, he straightened his coat and started towards Edison's table, with a slightly hesitant Matthew in tow.

As they approached, Jedidiah cleared his throat politely, catching Edison's attention. "Mr. Edison, I apologize for the intrusion. My name is Jedidiah Davenport, and this is Matthew Colton. We're great admirers of your work."

Edison, slightly surprised but not displeased, extended a hand. "Pleasure to meet you, gentlemen."

"Jedidiah is an inventor like you, Mr. Edison!" Matthew suddenly spoke up, to the slight embarrassment of his friend.

"Matthew!" Jedidiah Davenport blushed slightly and modestly replied, "I dabble a little..."

"Well, then this is definitely a pleasure!" Edison smiled greatly. "It's always fascinating meeting fellow inventors and discussing new ideas!"

Jedidiah turned his attention to the young European, who had been observing quietly. "And who might your companion be, Mr. Edison?"

"This is Nikola Tesla, a young inventor from Europe. He's got some fascinating ideas," Edison replied, a hint of respect in his voice.

Jedidiah, unfamiliar with Tesla, offered a polite but less enthusiastic greeting. "Pleasure to meet you, Mr. Tesla."

Tesla nodded in response, his expression modest yet confident. "The pleasure is mine, gentlemen. I am here to learn and to share ideas."

The conversation briefly turned to the convention and the advancements in technology being showcased. Jedidiah shared his plans to meet with Phineas B. Hargroves and discuss with him the aspects of airship technology.

Edison showed genuine interest, while Tesla listened intently, his eyes gleaming with curiosity.

After a few minutes of engaging discussion, Jedidiah and Matthew excused themselves, leaving the table with new thoughts swirling in their heads. As they walked away, Jedidiah whispered to Matthew, "Imagine, meeting Thomas Edison himself! And that Tesla fellow, he seemed sharp. I wonder if we'll hear more about him in the future."

Matthew chuckled. "In this place, anything's possible, Jed."

After leaving the dining room, Jedidiah Davenport and Matthew Colton finally retired to their suite. It was on the top floor of the Grand Hotel. The room, a blend of luxury and comfort, was a welcome respite from their rugged journey. As they entered, they were greeted by a spacious common area, elegantly furnished with plush chairs and a velvet sofa, all arranged around a polished mahogany coffee table. The soft glow of oil lamps cast a warm, inviting light, contrasting with the cool night.

Jedidiah walked over to the large windows, pulling back the heavy drapes to reveal the twinkling lights of gas street lamps below. He couldn't help but glance upwards, where the shadow of the airship loomed just beyond view.

Matthew, meanwhile, explored the suite, opening doors to reveal two separate bedrooms, each a haven of comfort. With fine linens on the large beds and a peaceful ambiance, they promised a good rest.

Both young men said their goodnights and retired to their private rooms. Matthew had no problem falling asleep almost the moment his head hit the pillow.

Jedidiah, however, was just the opposite. Despite his fatigue, he found himself restless, his mind still racing with thoughts of the airship hovering just above their heads. He lay in bed, staring at the ceiling, the image of the airship etched in his mind. As the clock struck midnight, an impulsive decision took hold. He needed to see it up close.

Quietly, Jedidiah slipped out of bed and tiptoed across the common room. He gently opened the door and made his way to the roof access. The hotel was silent, with only the distant hum of the city's nightlife penetrating the walls.

On the roof, the cool night air greeted him, a refreshing contrast to the warmth of the suite. As his gaze shifted, he found himself looking at the magnificent airship, bathed in moonlight, its silhouette a testament to human ingenuity and daring. The hotel's roof offered a panoramic view of the city's twinkling lights, but Jedidiah's attention was fixated on the airship. It loomed above him, a behemoth of canvas and ropes, gently swaying in the breeze. Jedidiah approached it with a mix of reverence and awe, his eyes tracing its contours and the ropes anchoring it to the hotel.

Lost in the marvel of the airship, he was startled by the sudden crack of gunshots, jolting the quiet night. The sound seemed to come from the floor directly beneath him. Adrenaline pumping, Jedidiah's instincts kicked in. He rushed back towards the roof access, his heart pounding in his chest.

Descending the stairs two at a time, he reached

the hallway of their floor. The corridor was dimly lit, the eerie silence now broken by his heavy breathing. As he approached his suite, a dark figure dashed out of the room next door, fleeing with a haste that spoke of urgency and fear.

Jedidiah paused at the doorway of the neighboring room, his mind racing. With caution, he peeked inside. The room was in disarray, signs of a struggle evident. And there, on the floor, lay Phineas B. Hargroves!

CHAPTER VIII

A Twist of Fate

Jedidiah Davenport stood in shock, staring at the unconscious form of inventor Phineas B. Hargroves. After snapping out of his fog, Jedidiah bolted into the room, his mind racing with concern and confusion.

"Mr. Hargroves!" Jedidiah called out as he checked for a heartbeat. Phineas was alive but not showing any signs of awakening. The inventor continued to lie motionless, his breathing shallow. Jedidiah's hands hovered over him, unsure how to help but desperate to do something.

Suddenly, the door swung open again, this time with hotel security rushing in, followed by local deputies. The scene they encountered, with Jedidiah bent over the unconscious body of the celebrated inventor, was incriminating, to say the least.

"Step away from him!" barked the chief of

security, his hand instinctively resting on his gun. The deputies fanned out, their expressions a mix of alertness and caution.

Jedidiah, hands raised in a gesture of innocence, tried to explain, "I just came in... I found him like this!"

Despite his protests, the officers were taking no chances. Jedidiah was handcuffed and led out of the room amidst a throng of curious onlookers and murmuring guests. The whispers and pointed fingers followed him as he was escorted down the corridor.

The officers marched him briskly down the street, their stern faces illuminated by the flickering gas street lamps. The once lively and welcoming streets of Wichita now seemed alien and hostile. Passersby stopped to stare, whispering among themselves as Jedidiah passed, a mix of curiosity and judgment in their eyes. The walk to the Marshal's office was short, but each step weighed heavily on Jedidiah, his mind racing with worry and uncertainty about what awaited him.

Once inside, Jedidiah was forced to sit down across from Marshal Cromwell. The Marshal's expression was unreadable as he listened to Jedidiah's account of the night's events.

"So, let me get this straight," the Marshal said, flipping through the notes he had taken. "You were up on the roof planning to steal the airship when you heard the gunshots?"

"Yes!" Jedidiah replied without thinking.

"Aha!" Marshal Cromwell exclaimed triumphantly. "So the old man caught you and tried to stop you from stealing it, and you tried to kill him!"

"Yes..." Jedidiah suddenly realized what he had just agreed to and shouted, "No! That's not it at all!"

Marshal Cromwell said, "Come on, you just admitted to trying to steal the airship!"

Jedidiah shook his head in confusion, "I did no such thing!"

"Were you on the roof trying to steal the airship or not?" Marshal Cromwell pounded his fist on the desk.

"I was on the roof but I wasn't trying to steal it!" Jedidiah replied confidently. "I just wanted a closer look!"

Marshal Cromwell chuckled as he shook his head. "That's what they all say!"

"All?" Jedidiah suddenly looked more confused and asked, "How many people do you question about stealing airships?"

"Well, I..."

Before Marshal Cromwell could finish his sentence, a commotion outside signaled another development. The door swung open, and to Jedidiah's immense relief, Phineas B. Hargroves himself staggered in, supported by a couple of his associates. His face was pale, but his eyes were alert.

Hargroves took one look at Davenport and declared, "Marshal, this man is innocent!" His voice was firm despite his weakened state. "He had nothing to do with my attack. I'd recognize my assailant if I saw him, and it's not him!"

Jedidiah breathed a sigh of relief as his handcuffs were promptly removed, and apologies were made.

After being released, Jedidiah walked with Phineas B. Hargroves and his associates back to the hotel.

"Thank you for clearing my name, Mr. Hargroves!" Jedidiah Davenport thanked the eccentric older man.

"It was the least I could do, my dear boy!" Phineas replied. "I couldn't let an innocent man pay for the crimes of another!"

Upon reaching the top floor of the hotel, Phineas dismissed his associates to their room across the hall. He then turned to his suite and paused at the door, glancing towards Jedidiah with a weary but genuine smile, and said, "Mr. Davenport, after such a harrowing night, might I invite you in for a cup of tea?"

Jedidiah nodded appreciatively. "That would be great, thank you, Mr. Hargroves."

Inside the spacious suite, an air of comfort and elegance prevailed. Phineas led Jedidiah to a sitting area, where plush chairs surrounded a low table. The room was filled with various trinkets and papers, evidence of Phineas' inventive mind at work.

As Phineas busied himself with preparing tea, Jedidiah took a moment to absorb his surroundings. The shelves were lined with engineering books, alongside intricate models of airships and other mechanical wonders.

"Please, make yourself comfortable, Mr. Davenport," Phineas said as he brought over a tray with a steaming teapot and two cups. He poured the tea, its aroma a calming presence in the room.

Jedidiah accepted the cup and placed it on the low table in front of him. "Do you always travel with all your belongings?"

"Wherever I go I must always feel at home!" Phineas Hargroves replied simply, as he took a sip of his tea. "I must apologize for the chaos of tonight, and I must thank you for your concern. It's not every day one finds himself knocked out only to be rescued by a stranger."

Jedidiah chuckled lightly, "Well, Mr. Hargroves, I can't say it's how I planned my evening, but I'm just glad you're alright."

"Call me Phineas, please," the inventor insisted. "After tonight, I believe formalities can be safely set aside."

"Phineas, then," Jedidiah agreed. "I have to admit that I've only recently discovered your work. However, I must say, your airship is nothing short of remarkable!"

Phineas' eyes lit up at the mention of his work. "Ah, the airship! My pride and joy. A culmination of years of dreaming and hard work. I've received a lot of attention from it, especially with my recent trip around the world."

Jedidiah nodded. "Actually, that's the main reason I'm here in Wichita. I'm looking to embark on a similar venture."

"You plan to take a trip around the world?" Phineas asked curiously.

Jedidiah finished his tea and placed the cup back down. "Not exactly," he began to explain about the situation he was going through and the trouble with the railroad. "I have a ten thousand acre ranch and over a thousand head of cattle. I can't afford to split my property down the middle!"

"And you say they've been cutting off your access roads for your freight company?" Phineas seemed genuinely interested. "I can understand your frustrations but I fail to see where I can help you."

Jedidiah leaned forward and simply stated, "Elijah Perkins may have taken control of the road but he can't control the skies!"

"Oh well, my dear boy, I'm afraid that the Icarus is not for sale!" Phineas Hargroves replied.

"The Icarus?" The young entrepreneur asked confused.

Phineas laughed as he explained that it was the name of his airship.

"I didn't think it would be," Jedidiah admitted. "I was hoping you'd sell me a copy of your blueprints."

The eccentric older man suddenly began to smile as he said, "That's actually one of my reasons for attending this convention." Phineas stood up and walked over to a large chest in the corner of the room. After placing a key in the lock and opening it, he reached in and produced a rolled-up sheet of paper. "I am looking to sell my plans."

"You're willing to part with the blueprints of your ship?" Jedidiah was taken by surprise, as he thought it was going to be harder to talk Mr. Hargroves into parting with his design.

"Well a copy of them." He replied as he sat back down. "I have no intention of building more ships, but I do want to get my original blueprint in case I need it for repairs."

"That's understandable!" Jedidiah exclaimed as he began to fidget in anticipation of laying his hands on the object in question.

Phineas started to hand them over and then suddenly withdrew them. "There is one stipulation..."

Jedidiah took a deep breath and sighed, "What's the catch?"

"You must also purchase the patent from me!" The older man leaned back in his chair and began to smile. "I plan to never work again and with the sale of both the patent and the design I can continue to travel the world for the rest of my life!"

Normally very free with his money, Jedidiah leaned back and thought about it for a moment. This was beginning to sound like a very expensive business venture. Finally, he decided to muster up the courage and ask how much. Phineas B. Hargroves quoted him a number that made the young entrepreneur wince.

After noticing the hesitation in his eyes, Phineas spoke up and said, "If you're not interested, I'm sure I won't have any trouble selling it to any number of individuals in attendance this weekend."

Realizing he would have to take out a loan and use his ranch and cattle as collateral, Jedidiah reluctantly extended his hand and said, "It's a deal!"

"Excellent you can have the bank draft written up and given to me when I arrive at your ranch!" The older man exclaimed. "I do hope you have comfortable quarters for me to stay in while I'm there."

"You're staying at my home?" Jedidiah blinked several times in confusion.

Phineas smiled as he said, "My dear boy, for the price you're paying, you're also getting me to help supervise the construction of your ship!"

This unexpected news actually made Jedidiah feel better. Not only would he have the blueprints but he would have the inventor himself there to make sure everything was done correctly.

Phineas handed over the plans and said, "I have obligations to be here until tomorrow evening." The older man paused for a moment as he turned and glanced at the clock mounted on the wall behind him. "Perhaps I should say today!" he laughed heartily. "I didn't realize it was nearly two-thirty in the morning!"

"Well, you know what they say about time flying when you're having fun..." Jedidiah laughed ironically as he remembered the hilarious time he spent in the Marshal's office.

"You're welcome to spend the day at the convention as my guest, and we can fly out first thing Monday morning and be there in time for breakfast!"

Jedidiah thought long and hard about this idea. If he left on horseback, he'd spend the entire day in the saddle, only to return late that evening. He couldn't accomplish anything by doing that. On the other hand, if he stayed at the convention and rode back by airship, he'd be home Monday morning without really losing any valuable work time at the ranch. 'Sounds like a good idea!' he exclaimed. Once again, he shook Mr. Hargroves' hand and then exited the room with his copy of the blueprints.

Back in his suite, Jedidiah found Matthew still asleep in his room. He had slept through everything. Jedidiah turned on his heel and retired to his room and tried to get some rest. His mind was preoccupied with the deal he had just made and its implications for his ranch. Since he couldn't sleep anyway, Jedidiah decided to look over the schematics for the airship he had spent so much money to acquire. What was supposed to be just a few minutes turned into a few hours. As Jedidiah noticed the sun coming up through his window, he decided it would be best if he laid down and got a little bit of rest before he started the day.

Just as Jedidiah had finally managed to doze off, the door to his room slammed open with a bang. Startled awake, he saw Matthew standing there, brimming with energy and cheerfulness.

"Rise and shine, Jed!" Matthew announced with a grin. "It's time to start the day. Don't be a lazy bones!"

In a half-asleep daze, Jedidiah grabbed the nearest pillow and tossed it in Matthew's direction. The pillow flew across the room and hit Matt in the side of the head. A look of puzzlement spread across his face.

"What did I say?" Matthew asked, genuinely

Jedidiah studied the schematics for hours until he noticed the sun coming through his window.

confused.

****

Later that day at the convention, Jedidiah and Matthew wandered through the exhibitions, but Jedidiah's thoughts were elsewhere. They observed the marvels of innovation surrounding them. Yet, Jedidiah's mind repeatedly drifted to his ranch, the airship project, and the looming conflict with Elijah Perkins. Matthew, sensing his friend's preoccupation, kept the conversation light, focusing on the displays and the potential of their upcoming venture.

Their interactions with Phineas were limited but cordial, with the inventor occasionally introducing them to other prominent figures. Despite the fascinating environment, Jedidiah felt an undercurrent of urgency, a longing to return to his ranch and confront the challenges awaiting him.

As the convention drew to a close, Jedidiah's anticipation for the journey ahead grew. He had a brief conversation with Phineas about the logistics of their travel. "We'll be flying over the fields and plains to reach your ranch," Phineas explained, his eyes gleaming with excitement. "You'll see the world like never before."

That evening, Jedidiah and Matthew retired

early. Their minds were occupied with thoughts of the next day's journey. Jedidiah lay in his bed, staring at the ceiling. He envisioned the airship soaring over his land, a symbol of defiance and hope against the looming threats.

****

Monday morning, with the rising sun casting a golden hue over the city, Phineas ascended to the hotel roof, where the airship was ready for departure. As the two associates he had hired to assist him over the weekend finished loading his belongings onboard the Icarus, he thanked them, gave them their pay, and told them they were no longer needed.

Jedidiah and Matthew were down the street at the stables retrieving their horses and the rifle that Jedidiah had left there. Once this was completed they headed out for a short ride to a field on the edge of town. It was there that they had arranged to meet Phineas B. Hargroves. He had landed his vessel only moments before their arrival.

As the two men dismounted and led their horses aboard, Jedidiah felt a surge of excitement mixed with apprehension. Phineas suggested they cover their horses' eyes with a cloth to keep them from getting anxious once they took off. After this was done, the airship lifted gently, and Wichita slowly receded below them.

Looking down at the shrinking landscape, Jedidiah felt a sense of liberation. The troubles with Perkins and the railroad seemed distant, if only for a moment. As the airship sailed smoothly through the sky, Jedidiah knew that they were not just heading back to his ranch but also towards a future filled with unknown challenges and possibilities.

The trip went along smoothly as they watched the scenery continue to whoosh past below them. They had been traveling for almost an hour when suddenly the calm was replaced with panic as the sounds of gunfire rang out from below them. Bullets whizzed past them, one of them striking the side of the airbag!

CHAPTER IX

Perils in the Sky

A faint hiss, like a whisper against the wind, caught Jedidiah Davenport's attention. His eyes widened as he realized the sound was gas escaping from the airship's bag. "Phineas!" he called out, alarm evident in his voice. "We've been hit!"

"Where did the shots come from?" Matthew Colton frantically ducked down. He dashed over to the side of the ship and precariously peeked over the edge.

Phineas B. Hargroves, hastily grabbing his telescope, peered through the lens, his face tensing as he spotted the source of their peril. "Blast it! The shots are coming from down there!" He handed the telescope over to Jedidiah and pointed towards the source of the gunfire.

"I bet they're from the railroad!" Jedidiah exclaimed.

"I don't think so!" Phineas Hargroves replied, as

he reached over and took the telescope back. "They're the two men who assaulted me in my hotel room the other night."

"Two men?" Jedidiah was confused. "I only saw one man run from your room."

"The other one had already gone downstairs to distract my two associates." Phineas started to tell the full details of what happened that night but was suddenly interrupted as another bullet went whizzing by him. "Listen, my boy, perhaps we can stroll down memory lane another time!"

"You're right. We've got to do something. We're losing altitude!" Jedidiah's voice wavered with a mix of concern and determination. The airship, once a symbol of their freedom, now seemed a precarious vessel, vulnerable to the elements and the hostilities below.

The older man shouted, "I've got to plug that hole!" as he made a mad dash for a nearby chest. "I've got something in here I can use to repair it!" Without hesitation, he grabbed hold of one of the cables attaching the canvas-covered airbag to the ship and began a perilous climb up the side. "Cover me!" Phineas shouted at Matthew and Jedidiah. His movements were swift but measured, each step a calculated risk against the swaying of the airship.

Without hesitation, Matthew grabbed Jedidiah's rifle, a piece of advanced technology in an era of simpler weapons. Equipped with a high-powered scope and range finder, it was Jedidiah's pride and now their crucial line of defense. Matthew steadied his aim, squinting as he focused on the two figures below. His finger tensed on the trigger, poised to protect them from further danger.

His attention shifted to the horses tied to a bush near their attackers. Taking a calculated shot, Matthew fired at the ground around the animals. The bullets hitting the earth startled the horses. Spooked, they strained against their restraints. With a final tug, they broke free and bolted into the woods at a full gallop.

Meanwhile, Jedidiah, though untrained in piloting, took the helm. He had observed Phineas steering the ship and attempted to mimic his actions. His hands gripped the controls tightly, trying to keep the ship steady in the sky. The task was daunting, more so with the ship gradually losing gas and Phineas' weight shifting on the side of the airbag.

Bullets whizzed past them, a dangerous reminder of the threat looming below. Jedidiah ducked instinctively, his heart pounding. The situation was dire. They were a floating target in the open sky.

Phineas started working his way towards the damaged area, his body swaying perilously with each gust of wind. Below, Matthew kept a vigilant watch, firing carefully timed shots to keep their attackers at bay. The tension was thick, each second stretching into eternity as they fought to stay afloat and safe. Jedidiah, navigating the airship with growing confidence, maneuvered to avoid the incoming fire, all while keeping a watchful eye on Phineas' progress.

In those moments, high above the earth, the three men faced a battle against the elements, against their assailants, and the odds. The airship, a beacon of innovation and hope, now bore the scars of their struggle. It was a testament to their resilience and determination to overcome the dangers that lay in their path.

Phineas B. Hargroves moved with the agility of a man half his age. The gas hissed out from a small puncture, a sinister whisper against the backdrop of the sky. Phineas finally reached the site of the damage. With deft hands, he pulled out a small roll of thick, rubberized canvas from his tool belt, a material designed specifically for emergency airship repairs. He spread a layer of quick-setting adhesive around the edges of the puncture, a special concoction of his own creation that could seal and withstand the pressure differences at high altitudes.

The airship lurched as another bullet zipped by, causing Phineas to grip the ropes tightly. His focus, however, never wavered. He carefully placed the patch over the hole, pressing it firmly into place.

The adhesive reacted quickly, forming a bond that halted the escape of gas almost instantly.

With the patch secured, Phineas took a small handheld stitching tool, a modified version of a sailmaker's palm, and began reinforcing the patch with a series of tight, overlapping stitches. Each stitch was precise, ensuring that the patch would hold under the strain of the flight.

As Phineas worked, his brow furrowed in concentration, and the danger they were in became more obvious. The patch job was a temporary solution, a race against time and the elements. Below, Matthew's sharpshooting provided them with the much-needed cover, while Jedidiah struggled to maintain control of the airship, now more unstable due to the shifting weight and the loss of gas.

Finally, Phineas tied off the last stitch, giving the patch a final, firm pat. He looked down and shouted, "I've done it!" The older man immediately slid down the ropes and dropped onto the deck.

"Take the wheel!" Jedidiah screamed as he saw Hargroves running towards him.

"No time!" Phineas replied in haste. "Keep it steady!" Without saying another word he ran into the cabin behind Davenport and started turning valves. There was an immediate sound of gas rushing back into the airbag from the emergency supply tanks. Within moments, the airship began to gain altitude. It drifted up and out of the range of the gunfire.

Realizing they were out of danger, everyone was finally able to take a sigh of relief.

"Take the wheel?" Jedidiah once again offered to step back and let the more experienced man take control.

Phineas merely smiled as he clasped the younger man's shoulder. "My dear boy, you're going to be piloting your own vessel soon. You might as well start learning now!"

Jedidiah hesitated slightly but then realized his newfound mentor was indeed correct. After being shown the compass near the Captain's wheel and how to navigate using the map, he began to feel more confident. Phineas was so impressed with his piloting skills that he retired into his sleeping quarters and took a nap for the remainder of the flight.

The next two hours went by uneventfully and soon they were floating high above the Davenport ranch. Needless to say, this caused quite a stir from the men working below. As they floated over Jedidiah's large stately manor, the shadow from the vessel caught the attention of the two servants inside.

"We having an eclipse today?" Pat Bennington glanced out the window as the light coming from it grew dim.

"What are you talking about, you old fool?" Agatha Porter furrowed her brow and shook her head. "It's probably just a storm cloud!" As she said this, she opened the back door and stepped outside. Glancing up at the sky, she immediately began to scream at the top of her lungs and rushed back in.

"What's the matter?" Pat asked, slightly confused, as the housekeeper ran past him. He too stepped outside and looked up at the sky. "Land o' Goshen!" he exclaimed. "We're being invaded!"

Pat immediately turned on his heel and ran inside. He was almost knocked flat on his back as Agatha Porter rushed into the kitchen armed with two shotguns. She tossed one to the portly cook and shouted, "Don't just stand there! We've got to defend the house!"

The two servants ran outside and began shooting towards the airship floating above them. Fortunately, they were out of range and weren't able to hit it, especially not with the weapons they were using.

After hearing the shots, Matthew once again grabbed the rifle with the high-powered scope and range finder. "We're under attack, again!" He shouted.

"That's impossible!" Jedidiah responded holding his course steady towards the area of the ranch where the fire had taken place a few nights ago. "There's no way they could have made it here as

The two servants ran outside and began shooting towards the airship floating above them.

fast as we have. Besides, you said you ran their horses off!"

"I can't explain it! I..." Matthew cut his sentence short as he trained the scope in the direction of the gunfire. He started laughing as he saw Jedidiah's two servants frantically waving around double-barrel shotguns and trying in vain to blast them out of the sky.

"What's so funny?" Jedidiah asked, glancing at his friend as if he had just lost his mind.

"You'll never guess who's shooting at us!" Matthew Colton continued laughing.

"Who?"

"Pat Bennington and Agatha Porter," Matthew howled, "your cook and housekeeper!"

"They must think we're from the railroad!" Jedidiah mused upon hearing this news, "or being invaded by visitors from another world..." he remarked to himself.

Realizing they were in no danger Jedidiah continued his path towards the recently refitted hay barn. "Matt!" He called out. "Do me a favor and go wake Phineas!"

"What for?" Matthew asked, confused.

"So he can show me how to land this thing!" Jedidiah laughed.

Minutes later, Jim Davis and half a dozen hired men came rushing out of the building and circled the vessel just as Jedidiah Davenport, with the aid of Phineas B. Hargroves, landed it parallel to the massive building.

"Hold your fire!" the ranch foreman shouted to his men upon spotting Jedidiah Davenport and Matthew Colton standing aboard the strange flying contraption. He immediately waved at the owner of the ranch letting him know it was safe to step down.

Jedidiah and Matthew immediately opened the door and slid out the ramp they had previously used to bring their animals aboard the ship. After removing the horses' blindfolds, they led them off the ship.

"Jed!" Jim Davis exclaimed. "What is this thing and who is that?" Jim suddenly noticed the eccentric figure of Phineas B. Hargroves standing on the deck of the strange vessel.

"It's hard to explain..." Jedidiah replied. "But Matthew can provide you with all the details!" He turned and patted his childhood friend on the back.

Matthew's eyes widened upon hearing this, and he exclaimed, "I'm still not completely sure what's going on myself!"

"Don't worry, you'll do just fine!" He handed Matthew the blueprints and turned back to Jim Davis. "I may just have a way to tip this war with the railroad. Those plans I just gave Matt are the key." He turned and pointed towards Phineas Hargroves. "Make sure you follow his instructions to the letter!"

Jim's eyes widened in disbelief as he watched Davenport mount his horse. "Where are you going?"

"I've got some explaining to do to a couple of homestead defenders!" Jedidiah called over his shoulder as he started riding in the direction of his Victorian manor.

Upon reaching the towering impressive structure he called a house, Jedidiah was immediately greeted by the sounds of gunshots. "Hold your fire!" He shouted. "It's me!"

Agatha Porter instantly came rushing out with Pat Bennington waddling along behind her.

"Thank goodness you're back!" The older woman shouted in relief. "You'll never believe what just floated by and tried to blow up the whole house!"

Jedidiah tilted his head and tried to contain his laughter as he asked, "What just floated by and tried to blow up the house?"

"You should have seen it, Jed!" Pat exclaimed, his round face lit up under his beard. "It was like something out of that Jowls Burns novel!"

"Oh yes... Jowls Burns..." Jedidiah was finding it even more difficult not to laugh. "Author of such popular novels as Around the Barn in Eighty Bales and Twenty Thousand Leaps 'Cross the Creek."

"What?"

"I think you meant Jules Vernes..."

"Well, whatever his name is!" Pat shouted. "We had little green men dropping out of the sky all around us. You would have lost the house for sure if it hadn't been for the two of us fighting them off side by side!" He turned to Agatha Porter and tried to put his arm around her shoulders, but she immediately elbowed him in the ribs and stepped to the side.

"Well, that's not exactly how it happened..." She looked at the other servant with disdain and then said, "But we did manage to scare it off... whatever it was!"

It was at this point that Jedidiah couldn't contain himself any longer. After having a well-needed, stress-relieving laugh, he began to explain to them about the airship and his recent trip to Wichita.

"Land o' Goshen!" Pat exclaimed. "So you were the one soaring above us?"

"Well, not just me, Matt and Professor Hargroves were up there as well!"

Pat's face suddenly took on an arrogant boastful expression as he turned and looked at his coworker. "And you thought we were being invaded by otherworldly beings!"

"Oh yes..." Agatha scoffed. "And you were perfectly calm the entire time!"

"Well, one of us had to retain a cool head!" He nodded, insufferably pleased with himself.

Jedidiah shook his head and chuckled as he told his cook he had better retire to the kitchen before Agatha hit him over the head with something. "We're going to have another guest staying for a while, so be prepared to make extra food!" he called out after the portly servant.

"What's this about another guest?" Agatha asked, confused.

Jedidiah took the time to explain how Phineas Hargroves would be staying with them until the airship was complete, he remounted his horse and prepared to ride into town.

Agatha Porter looked even more confused, as she stepped onto the porch and asked, "Where are you going now?"

"Spoon Fork!" he called out. "Gotta make arrangements for Phineas' payment!"

The town in question was about an hour's ride from his ranch. The journey went by uneventfully, much to his relief. After arriving on the dusty streets, he directed his horse straight to the local bank. His arrival drew attention from a small group of men gathered inside The Rusty Nail Saloon.

Jedidiah had just dismounted his horse and tied the reins to the hitching post when he heard someone from behind him call his name.

"Hold it!" One of several men shouted. "We want to talk to you!"

Jedidiah gasped as they surrounded him!

CHAPTER X

Securing The Future

Jedidiah Davenport turned in circles, his gaze sweeping over the group that surrounded him in the center of Spoon Fork. He recognized familiar faces: Luther Caldwell, the savvy saloon owner; Jacob Harrington, the town's skilled blacksmith; Horace McKinley, who operated the telegraph office; Henry Porter, owner of the general store and an acquaintance of Jedidiah; and Gideon Stewart, another general store owner.

"What's the meaning of this?" Jedidiah asked, suspiciously. "Are you here to try and run me out of town?"

"Jed, it's not like that!" Henry Porter stepped forward as the spokesman of the group. "We had a meeting Sunday morning and discussed a few things..."

****

Twenty-four hours earlier, in the dimly lit room of The Rusty Nail, a group of Spoon Fork's prominent businessmen gathered around an old oak table. The air was heavy with tension and the faint aroma of whiskey. Luther Caldwell, the saloon owner, leaned against the bar, his eyes surveying the gathered faces.

Jacob Harrington, the blacksmith, broke the silence. "We need to talk about what's happening with Davenport and the railroad," he said, his voice gruff but tinged with concern.

Luther nodded. "I know we all agreed to support Perkins' plan for the railroad, but things are getting out of hand. That explosion at Jedidiah's office was too far."

Horace McKinley, the telegraph operator, adjusted his spectacles. "I agree. We thought the railroad would be good for business, but I never signed up for violence."

Henry Porter, owner of one of the general stores, shifted uncomfortably. "The pressure from Perkins was one thing, but seeing Jedidiah continue to get hurt over and over again... I don't know if I can be part of this anymore."

Gideon Stewart, from the other general store, sighed. "But think about the business the railroad could bring. We're struggling as it is."

Jacob clenched his fists. "What's the point of

Spoon Fork's prominent businessmen
gathered around an old oak table.

more business if it means turning on one of our own? Jed's been nothing but good to this town."

Luther poured himself a drink. "I've watched Jedidiah grow his business from nothing. The kid's got guts!"

Horace peered at the group. "We may have been pushed into this by Perkins, but it's time we decide where we stand, with or without the railroad."

The room fell silent as each man contemplated the weight of their decisions. The allure of progress was now shadowed by the reality of their actions.

Henry finally spoke, his voice low. "We started this thinking about the future of Spoon Fork, but maybe we lost sight of what that means. It's not just about business. It's about community too."

Gideon nodded slowly. "Maybe we did get carried away. Perhaps it's time we rethink our stance."

Luther raised his glass. "To Spoon Fork and to doing what's right, even if it's hard."

The men raised their glasses in a somber toast, each lost in thought about the future and the challenging path that lay ahead.

****

"After a little more discussion, we came to a unanimous decision to stand by your side no matter what!" Henry Porter declared.

Jedidiah was at a loss for words. He leaned back against the hitching post in front of the bank and breathed a sigh of relief, nodding as he looked down at the ground. Glancing back up at the faces of the men around him, he asked, "You mean it?"

"Jed, we all owe you an apology!" Henry continued to speak for the group. "We all let greed blind us from the things that truly matter." He turned and looked at Gideon Stewart, who gave him a nod of approval. "Gideon and I have decided to let you have the supplies you need."

The other store owner spoke up, "We've already arranged for them to be sent out to your ranch today!" He quickly added, "They'll be added to your account, and you can pay whenever you get the chance!"

"Doggone you, Gideon!" Henry whirled around furiously at the other man. "Did you have to bring that up right this minute?"

"Doggone me?" Gideon's eyes showed his confusion then his frustration. "Doggone you, Hank Porter! We agreed to support Jedidiah but never said anything about going broke to do it!"

Henry Porter nodded in agreement but quickly stated, "There's a time and a place for things like that, and this ain't it!"

Jedidiah laughed and began to wave his hands in front of himself to get the two men's attention. "It's fine, I didn't expect to get the supplies for free," he said. Dropping his head for a moment and then looking back up, he added, "I don't know when I'll be able to pay you, though. If I don't get my freight company fully functioning again soon, I'll..."

"Just take your time, Jed!" Hank replied. "We just wanted you to know you have the support of the town behind you once again!"

With that being said, the group dispersed and went back to their respective places of business.

Once inside the bank, Jedidiah spotted Mr. Clayton from the main branch of the Davenport Dispatch & Delivery Company making a deposit.

"Jed!" the older man exclaimed. "Thank goodness you're here!"

Jedidiah approached Mr. Clayton, noting the concern etched on his face. "What's the matter, Clayton? You look like you've seen a ghost."

Clayton sighed heavily, running his hand through his hair. "It's the deliveries, Jed. We've been having more trouble than I care to admit. Perkins' men are making it impossible for us to operate efficiently. Several more routes have been sabotaged, and our drivers are scared."

Jedidiah's jaw clenched at this news. "Sabotaged? In what way?"

"More roadblocks, threatening messages, and a couple of our wagons have been damaged beyond repair. It's as if they know our every move,"

Clayton explained, frustration clear in his voice. "It's not just our branch, we've been receiving telegraphs from all branches within a thirty-mile radius!"

"At least they're not attacking the extended branches, only the local ones." Jedidiah breathed a small sigh of relief. "I couldn't imagine if all twenty-five locations were shut down!"

Mr. Clayton nodded his head in agreement. "Thank goodness for small favors!" He replied.

"Alright, Clayton. I need you to send out telegraphs to all the managers of the branches that have been under attack and have them meet me in your office first thing Wednesday morning. It's time we change our strategy."

Clayton nodded. "Will do, Jed. I'll get the word out."

As Clayton was preparing to leave, the bank manager, Mr. Theodore Simmons, approached Davenport and asked him if he needed any help. Jedidiah asked if he could speak to him alone in his office. They walked a few feet away and closed the door behind them.

After he sat down across from the manager, Jedidiah explained his need for a substantial loan. "It's for a project that will ensure the future of the Davenport Dispatch & Delivery Company," he stated confidently.

Mr. Simmons adjusted his glasses and examined

the face of the young entrepreneur before him. "You've always been as good as your word, Jed. What kind of project are we talking about?"

Jedidiah unrolled another copy of the airship's blueprints. "This, Mr. Simmons. This is our future."

Mr. Simmons' eyes widened as he took in the details of the schematics. "An airship?" he exclaimed, a mix of surprise and intrigue evident in his voice. "This is ambitious, Jed. Very ambitious."

"I know it is. But it's also necessary. With this, we can bypass all the roadblocks and interference from Perkins and his railroad. We'll be transporting goods through the air."

Simmons leaned back in his chair, pondering. "This will require a significant amount of capital, Jed. Are you sure about this?"

"I've never been more certain about anything in my life," Jedidiah replied with a steadfast gaze. "I'm willing to put my ranch up as collateral."

After a lengthy discussion, Simmons agreed to the loan, impressed by Jedidiah's vision and determination. Simmons expedited the processing allowing Jedidiah to leave with the bank draft that would enable him to build the airship and revolutionize his business.

As he walked out of Mr. Simmons' office, Jedidiah bumped into Mr. Clayton, who was still standing outside the door. He was slightly surprised to see him there. "Have you got a response already from the telegraphs?" Jedidiah asked the manager and dispatcher of his main branch.

"Not yet, Jed!" Mr. Clayton replied quickly. "You didn't tell me what time to have them be here!"

"As early as possible!" Davenport exclaimed. "We'll start the meeting at eight am sharp!"

"Good idea!" Mr. Clayton turned on his heel and started for the exit. "The earlier the better!"

After being handed the bank draft by one of the tellers, Jedidiah Davenport stepped into the street. He immediately felt the weight of his decision. Jedidiah was putting everything on the line for a chance at a future free from Perkins' control. But with the support of the townspeople and his newfound ally in Phineas B. Hargroves, he felt a surge of hope. The airship was more than a business venture. It was a symbol of defiance, a testament to his resolve to protect his legacy.

It was still early morning as Jedidiah mounted his horse and headed back to his ranch. The excitement of the airship's arrival had settled into a buzz of activity. Phineas B. Hargroves, with his eccentric charisma, had quickly become a figure of intrigue among the ranch hands. Plans for the construction of Jedidiah's own airship were already underway, with workers gathering to discuss the logistics and materials needed.

Jedidiah didn't waste any time in joining

everyone at the new airship hangar. Privately, he handed over the bank draft to Phineas Hargroves, who in turn presented Jedidiah with the patent for the airship design.

"How long do you think it will take to construct the airship?" Jedidiah asked the eccentric older man.

"Took me three years to build mine," Phineas replied, simply.

"Years?" Jedidiah's eyes grew wide with anxiety.

In a calming voice, Hargroves said, "My dear boy that's because I was designing and working out the bugs as I went. Also, I had very little help in building mine. You practically have an entire army!"

Jedidiah breathed another sigh of relief. "So how long do you think?"

Phineas thought about it for a moment before saying, "Any average person can have this done in six months to a year!"

"I don't have six months to a year…"

"Then fortunately for you, I'm not an average person!" Phineas B. Hargroves began to boast about himself. "I can get it done for you in six weeks."

"I need it in three!"

"That would take a miracle worker…" Phineas replied as he feigned shock. "Fortunately for you, my dear boy, I just happen to be a miracle worker!"

"You'll have it done in three weeks?" Jedidiah asked, pleased.

Phineas thought about it for a moment and then said, "Make it a month! That'll give me an extra week for unexpected incidents!"

"Fair enough!" Jedidiah exclaimed as he shook the eccentric man's hand.

"One other thing, Jedidiah." Phineas Hargroves called out before the young man could leave. "I happened to notice that you have the roof of this building rigged to open up when the time comes to release your airship."

"That's the plan…"

"Bravo for ingenuity, my dear boy!" The older man suddenly looked puzzled as he asked, "What do you plan to power the crank and pull system to conduct such a feat?"

"Ah, my dear Professor, that's a secret I will reveal when the time comes!"

As Jedidiah turned to leave the airship hangar, Matthew Colton approached him with a hint of concern on his face. "Jed, there's something I need to tell you. It's about Jim Davis."

"Is he hurt?" Jedidiah asked, suddenly becoming concerned. "Was there another attack on the ranch while I was gone?"

"Nothing like that," Matthew assured him. "It's just that he took off not long after you left and hasn't been back since."

Jedidiah paused, his brow furrowing slightly. "He's probably just making sure the ranch is secure, riding the range, you know how thorough he is."

Matthew shuffled his feet, his expression uneasy. "I thought so too, but I saw him heading towards town, not the range."

This revelation struck a chord in Jedidiah's mind, bringing forth a memory he had almost forgotten in the whirlwind of recent events. The watch was found in the debris of the explosion – an item that could potentially unravel a mystery.

A mix of suspicion and concern washed over Jedidiah. Jim's sudden departure to town, especially at such a crucial time, was out of character. "I need to find out what he's up to," Jedidiah muttered, more to himself than to Matthew.

Mounting his horse, Blaze, once again, Jedidiah set off towards Spoon Fork. The airship's construction was in more than capable hands. This unexpected turn of events with Jim demanded his immediate attention.

As he rode into town, Jedidiah's mind raced with possibilities. Was Jim involved in something shady or underhanded? Could he possibly be in league with Perkins? The uncertainty gnawed at him. Jim wasn't just an employee. He was a trusted friend and an integral part of Davenport's operation

Jedidiah's eyes scanned the streets, searching

for any sign of Jim Davis. The town, bustling with activity, offered no immediate clues. He decided to start at The Rusty Nail, a place where information flowed as freely as the whiskey.

Pushing through the saloon doors, Jedidiah's presence drew a few curious glances. He walked straight to the bar, his gaze steady and purposeful.

"Luther, have you seen Jim around?" he asked the saloon owner.

Luther wiped down a glass before responding. "Saw him earlier; seemed in a hurry. Headed towards the outskirts of town, if I'm not mistaken."

Thanking Luther, Jedidiah left the saloon, his concern deepening. The outskirts of town were an area where one could find both solitude and secrecy. Determined, Jedidiah spurred his horse in that direction, his mind ablaze with questions and the faint, unsettling ember of betrayal.

As Jedidiah guided his horse through the bustling streets of Spoon Fork, he caught sight of Sheriff Thompson near the town's small post office. The sheriff was a man of stern countenance but fair judgment. However, Jedidiah knew that divulging too much could lead to unwanted scrutiny concerning Jim Davis, whom the sheriff was already regarding with a wary eye.

"Sheriff Thompson," Jedidiah called out as he approached, waving his hand in greeting.

"Jed!" Sheriff Thompson waved back. "I haven't

seen you in a few days. Any more trouble out at your ranch?"

Jedidiah updated the Sheriff about the fire and his trip with Matthew to Wichita. He told him about purchasing the plans for the airship.

"Airship?" Sheriff Thompson seemed confused. "Never thought I'd see the day when men would be sailing around the skies in a ship."

Jedidiah smiled, a mix of pride and relief evident on his face. "Yes, it's something, isn't it? That's the work of Phineas B. Hargroves, a brilliant inventor from Wichita. We're collaborating on this project that will hopefully save my business."

The sheriff raised an eyebrow, his interest piqued. "How's this airship, as you say, going to help with your current predicaments?"

"It's a way to bypass the railroad blockades set up by Perkins and his men. We'll be transporting goods through the air, making it harder for them to interfere with my operations," Jedidiah explained, careful to keep his tone casual yet confident.

Sheriff Thompson nodded slowly, clearly impressed. "That's quite an ambitious plan, Jed. But if anyone can pull it off, it'd be you. Just be careful; you're treading on uncharted territory."

"I appreciate the concern, Sheriff," Jedidiah replied. "I'll be sure to tread cautiously."

After Jedidiah parted ways with Sheriff Thompson, he continued his search for his ranch foreman. He was just about to give up when he passed by an alley and heard voices. It sounded like a heated argument. Jedidiah dismounted his horse, cautiously made his way over, and peeked between the buildings. He gasped in horror as he spotted his foreman talking to none other than Elijah Perkins' number one henchman, Leroy Johnson!

CHAPTER XI

Shadows of Doubt

Jim Davis consorting with Leroy Johnson – Jedidiah couldn't believe his eyes! *"What's he doing talking to that scoundrel?"* he thought to himself. Before he could answer that question, he witnessed the two men mount their horses and ride off in separate directions. The dust kicked up by their horses' hooves seemed to hang in the air, mirroring Jedidiah's suspended state of disbelief. What connection could Jim, a man he trusted implicitly, have with Johnson, Elijah Perkins' notorious right-hand man?

Shaking off the shock of what he had just witnessed, Jedidiah made a decisive turn towards the sheriff's office. He led his horse down the street and tied it to the hitching post outside.

Upon entering, he spotted Sheriff Thompson behind his desk and his two deputies sitting at a nearby table. They were having a cup of coffee

Jim Davis consorting with Leroy Johnson!

while playing a game of checkers.

"Sheriff, I need to talk to you about something," Jedidiah said, as he glanced towards the deputies and then back at the sheriff.

Sheriff Thompson picked up on his signal, nodded his head, and said, "Eli! Wesley! How about the two of you finish that game later? I need both of you to go out and patrol the streets."

"Yes, Sir," they said in unison, promptly standing to their feet and leaving the room.

Turning back to Jedidiah, Sheriff Thompson motioned for him to have a seat at his desk. "Now tell me what's on your mind, Jed."

Jedidiah Davenport didn't waste any time telling Sheriff Thompson about seeing Jim Davis and Leroy Johnson in the alley together. The older man listened intently, his brows furrowing in concern. After a moment of contemplation, he asked, "But you couldn't hear what they were saying?"

Jedidiah sighed as he shook his head. "Not a word!"

The Sheriff thought about it for a moment and said, "Jed, you know my concerns about Jim. His pocket watch being found in the debris of the explosion at your freight office is mighty suspicious. Did you get a chance to ask him about it?"

"I did and he claims that it mysteriously went missing a few days prior."

"Uh-huh..." Sheriff Thompson nodded his head and replied, "That's certainly convenient..."

"You think he's lying?"

"I didn't say that..." The older man leaned back in his chair and casually offered some advice, "Jed, if he is involved in this, we need to know. However, if he doesn't know you suspect him, we could use that to our advantage. I can't tell you what to do but if it were up to me I wouldn't confront him about what you saw. I'd just keep an eye on him and see if he does anything else suspicious."

"I understand what you're saying, Sheriff, but part of me really wants to know why he was talking to Johnson."

Sheriff Thompson completely understood and nodded his head. "Only you can make that decision."

Jedidiah stood to his feet and started towards the door. "No matter what I decide, I'll keep you updated."

Returning to the ranch, Jedidiah was immediately drawn back into work. He immersed himself in the construction of the airship. The open fields of the ranch transformed into a bustling construction site, alive with the sounds of hammering, sawing, and the occasional shout of instruction. Inside the expansive building that once housed hay, the skeleton of the airship began to emerge, its framework a lattice of wood and metal, symbolizing not just a machine, but a collective dream taking physical form.

Phineas B. Hargroves, the mastermind behind the design, was a whirlwind of activity. His eccentric genius was evident in every precise instruction he gave, every piece of the airship he inspected. He moved among the workers, a conductor orchestrating a symphony of creation, his voice booming with enthusiasm and his eyes sparkling with the joy of creation. His wild hair and flamboyant attire only added to the aura of an inventor not just building a machine, but realizing a vision.

The rest of this day and the following day were both devoted strictly to the building of this vessel. Jedidiah found himself learning more than he ever expected about airship construction. He worked alongside the men, lifting, fitting, and securing parts under Phineas's guidance. Every bolt tightened and every beam placed brought them closer to their goal. The ranch hands, initially skeptical, grew increasingly invested in the project, their hard work fueled by the infectious energy of Phineas and Jedidiah's unwavering determination.

****

The night before the meeting with his local

branch managers, Jedidiah and Matthew sat on the front porch of Davenport's Victorian home, engaging in a deep conversation about the situation.

"Do you need me to go with you, tomorrow?" Matthew asked. "After all, I am the manager of your Sheffield branch."

"I want you to stay here and help Phineas oversee the construction of the airship." Jedidiah thought for a moment then added, "And keep an eye on Jim."

"You decided to take Sheriff Thompson's advice and not confront him?"

"I'm still thinking about it." Jedidiah confided in his childhood friend. "I still can't believe Jim would be mixed up with Johnson or Perkins either one."

"It is hard to believe," Matthew agreed, "because he's always been a good friend to both of us. Remember the time before I moved to Sheffield and the three of us were on that posse together?"

****

A few years earlier, Jedidiah Davenport, Matthew Colton, and Jim Davis found themselves on a perilous adventure. They were part of a posse, tasked with tracking down a notorious gang that had recently robbed a stagecoach and terrorized the local townsfolk.

Under the blazing sun, they rode hard through the dusty canyons, their determination unwavering. The outlaw gang was known for its cunning and ruthlessness, making the pursuit even more dangerous.

As they closed in on the outlaws' hideout, tension hung thick in the air. The three friends communicated with just a glance, their unspoken understanding a testament to years of friendship and shared experiences.

The three of them had volunteered to go around the back while Sheriff Thompson and the rest of the posse rode in from the front.

Suddenly, a barrage of gunfire erupted from behind a rocky outcrop. The outlaws had ambushed them, catching them off guard. Bullets whizzed by, kicking up dust and sending echoes through the canyon.

Matthew found himself pinned down, unable to return fire. An outlaw was closing in on him, hidden behind a large boulder. Just as the situation seemed dire, Jim sprang into action. With unparalleled accuracy, he took a shot, hitting the outlaw with precision, saving Matthew from a certain fate.

The outlaws, rattled by Jim's expert marksmanship and undaunted courage, quickly retreated, fleeing deeper into the canyon. Their ambush had failed, thanks to Jim's quick thinking and impeccable aim.

Matthew, shaken but grateful, looked at Jim with deep appreciation. "Jim, you saved my life. I owe you one!"

****

"He's definitely saved my life more than once," Jedidiah replied as he too remembered the events of that day. "There's got to be a reason why he was meeting with Johnson!"

"I'm sure you're right but what could it be?" Matthew agreed but also sat in bewilderment as to why the characteristically trustworthy Jim Davis would ever be seen with such a shady character.

It was about this time that Pat Bennington opened the front door, stepped outside, and rang his dinner bell. "Soup's on!" he shouted at the top of his lungs.

"Pat!" Jedidiah placed both hands over his ears and leaned over in the opposite direction of his portly servant. "We're the only two out here. Was that really necessary?"

Pat just started chuckling and said, "Just wanted to make sure I got your attention. That Phineas Hargroves fellow you invited to stay with us is already sitting down to grubs. You know how he eats and if the two of you don't come in soon there won't be any left!"

"Okay, okay!" Jedidiah laughed. "We'll be right in!"

"Don't forget to wash your hands!" Agatha Porter's voice could be heard coming from inside the house.

Jedidiah and Matthew both laughed and reassured her that they would.

After Pat was back inside the house and the door was closed, Jedidiah turned to Matthew and said, "I'll sleep on it tonight and decide what I'm going to do while I'm in town."

"That's a good idea!" Matthew agreed wholeheartedly. "Don't make any hasty decisions, and if he is mixed up in it, we'll find out what it is!"

The two of them stood up and went inside the house for a hearty meal with Pat, Agatha, and Phineas. Doing as they promised, they made sure to wash up before sitting down with the others.

****

The next day dawned early for Jedidiah as he rode into Spoon Fork for the critical meeting with his depot managers. The meeting room was filled with a sense of urgency. Despite the challenges, there was a shared determination to keep the business afloat.

The morning sun streamed through the windows as Jedidiah, with a stern yet hopeful expression, called the meeting to order. Mr. Clayton, his loyal manager from the main branch, sat to his right, his face etched with concern. Gathered around the rustic oak table were Lucas Benson from Sheffield, Clara Johnson from Hawthorn Grove, Thomas Reed from Birchfield, Sarah Hamilton from Meadowbank, and Owen Fisher from Riverside. Each carried the weight of their respective branches, their faces a mix of resolve and apprehension.

Jedidiah cleared his throat, drawing the room's attention. "Thank you all for making the journey here. We're facing a challenge unlike any before, and it's time we adapt our strategy."

Mr. Clayton nodded in agreement. "Perkins' men have forced our hand. We need new routes. Even if they are less efficient and take longer. We have to consider the safety of our drivers."

"Fortunately, none of the nineteen branches that extend beyond your towns have been affected," Jedidiah stated with a tone of relief. "At least not as of yet. Now each of you knows what routes have been interfered with that directly hinder your operations. I want to know what each of you plan to do about it and what steps you will take to accomplish it."

Lucas Benson leaned forward. "In Sheffield, we can divert through Miller's path. It's longer and rough, but it's off their radar."

Clara Johnson added, "Our priority in Hawthorn Grove is preserving our perishables. The north valley route is our best bet, despite the extra travel time."

Thomas Reed from Birchfield interjected, "We'll need to tread carefully on the old mining trails, but our wagons should make it through unharmed if we pack them right."

Sarah Hamilton of Meadowbank suggested, "The eastern hill route may be longer, but it's our safest option. We'll manage."

Owen Fisher from Riverside concluded, "We'll move smaller shipments more frequently through the backwoods path. It's not ideal, but it's necessary."

Jedidiah nodded, absorbing their input. "As Mr. Clayton has pointed out, our focus is safety and reliability, even if it means slowing down. We'll adjust schedules and manage client expectations accordingly."

Mr. Clayton agreed to oversee the transition, emphasizing the need for heightened security and vigilance.

Jedidiah stood, his eyes sweeping across the faces of his managers. "Your commitment during these trying times is invaluable. We'll meet again in two weeks to review our progress and adjust as needed. For now, let's stay strong and united."

As the meeting adjourned, the managers

dispersed, each carrying a new sense of purpose. Jedidiah remained, gazing at the maps sprawled across the table, contemplating the future. In these uncertain times, his resolve to protect his business and defy Perkins' control was more robust than ever.

After the meeting, Jedidiah chose to stay at the freight office, lending a hand in loading the wagons. The physical labor was a welcome distraction from his troubled thoughts, a reminder of the tangible aspects of his business that he could control.

He left the office and walked around the back of the building, into the very heart of his freight company. Under Davenport's expert direction, the workers moved with a sense of purpose, loading goods onto wagons with the practiced precision of seasoned professionals. Amidst the flurry of activity, a young man, about sixteen or seventeen years of age, caught Jedidiah's attention. Even though he had been intently staring at Jedidiah, he had been working harder than anyone else there, swiftly and efficiently handling the cargo with impressive diligence.

Approaching the newcomer with a friendly yet authoritative demeanor, Jedidiah extended a welcoming hand. "You're new here, aren't you? What's your name?"

The young man, slightly awestruck, replied,

"Tom, sir. Tom Miller. I've heard a lot about you, Mr. Davenport. They say you built all this from scratch."

A chuckle escaped Jedidiah's lips, and a spark of pride flickered in his eyes. "Well, Tom, it wasn't quite from scratch. My father started the freight company, but back then it was just one office and a couple of wagons. I took over when I was about your age."

He motioned towards the depot, alive with the sounds of commerce and progress. "It took a lot of hard work, strategic decisions, and a bit of luck to turn it into what it is today. Each one of these depots," he said, sweeping his hand across the horizon, "represents a step in that journey."

As Jedidiah returned to the thick of operations, memories flooded back – the early days of tireless work, the exhilaration of expansion, the sleepless nights spent strategizing over maps, and the sense of accomplishment in each successful venture. His heart swelled with the knowledge that every decision and every risk had culminated in this thriving network.

Observing Tom still lingering, captivated by the scene, Jedidiah couldn't help but share a piece of wisdom. "Stick around, Tom. There's a lot to learn, and if you're willing, I could use someone with your eagerness. This business is more than just wagons and goods, it's about seeing the potential in things and having the courage to chase it."

As the sun began to dip below the horizon, marking the end of another long day, Jedidiah rode back to the ranch. He had decided that a confrontation with Jim was inevitable, but the timing had to be right.

Upon arrival, he was about to seek out Jim when a sudden commotion at the construction site caught his attention. Dropping the reins of his horse, Jedidiah sprinted towards the source of the disturbance. As he neared, the sounds of panicked voices and urgent movement grew louder.

Rounding the corner of the barn, Jedidiah came to an abrupt halt. Before him was a scene of chaos —one of the newly constructed sections of the airship had collapsed!

CHAPTER XII

From The Ashes Rise

Jedidiah Davenport's heart thundered in his chest as he sprinted towards the collapsed section of the airship. The air was thick with dust and the sharp scent of splintered wood, overlaying the heavy aroma of sweat and fear, and the clamor of panicked voices and the desperate clatter of shifting debris filled the air, painting a scene of chaos and desperation.

As Jedidiah weaved through the frantic workers, Matthew Colton caught up with him. His face was pale, eyes wide with shock. "Jed! It just gave way, out of nowhere!" Matthew gasped, gesturing frantically towards the wreckage.

Jedidiah's gaze swept the scene, his mind racing. "Is anyone hurt?" he barked, scanning for injured workers amidst the chaos.

Matthew shook his head, his expression turning grave. "Most are accounted for, but..." His voice trailed off, hinting at a worse scenario, left unsaid.

Suddenly a muffled cry for help cut through the chaos. "Over here! I'm trapped!" the voice was unmistakable. It was Phineas B. Hargroves, laced with pain but unmistakably alive.

Without a moment's hesitation, Jedidiah plunged into the heart of the wreckage, his hands moving with frantic urgency, tearing away chunks of wood and twisted metal. Others joined him, fueled by his determination, working in unison to uncover their trapped comrade.

It was then that Jim Davis emerged from the crowd, his expression serious and focused. "Stand back!" he shouted, his eyes quickly assessing the situation. In his hands, he held a long, sturdy beam he planned to use as a makeshift lever.

Jim positioned the beam under a large piece of metal pinning Phineas down. Muscles straining, he levered the timber, creating a gap just wide enough to pull the older man out. "Now!" he shouted.

Jedidiah and a few others dove into the gap, their hands reaching for the injured inventor. They pulled Phineas free, his body limp but alive. A collective sigh of relief rose from the men as they laid him down safely away from the wreckage.

Jim didn't pause to celebrate. He quickly assessed the scene for more trapped workers, his actions efficient and focused. "We need to check for others. Carefully lift the debris and watch for any movement," his voice cut through the chaos.

Jedidiah found himself momentarily stunned by Jim's heroism. The man he had been so suspicious of was now the savior in their midst, his actions selfless and brave. The internal conflict within Jedidiah grew. This was the Jim Davis he knew. This man would never conspire with the likes of a lowlife like Leroy Johnson.

As the workers continued their rescue efforts, Jedidiah approached Jim, clapping him on the back. "That was quick thinking, Jim. You saved his life!"

Jim simply nodded, his expression still focused. "It's nothing any of you wouldn't have done for me."

Jedidiah's gaze lingered on Jim, a mix of gratitude and unresolved suspicion playing in his mind. The confrontation he had been contemplating now seemed less urgent, overshadowed by the day's events.

For the moment, Jedidiah decided to hold off on confronting Jim about his secret meeting with Johnson. There were more pressing matters at hand – the reconstruction of the airship and the safety of his crew.

After the commotion had finally died down and every man was accounted for, Jedidiah approached the eccentric inventor who appeared to be no worse for wear.

"Are you sure you're okay?" Jedidiah asked

with genuine concern.

"My dear boy, it will take far more than an airship falling on me to put me out of commission!" Hargroves chuckled as he turned to assess the damage. "I don't know what caused that support beam to give way, but I will find out!" Turning back to Jedidiah, he added, "Don't worry, this is not as bad as it looks. This shouldn't put us more than a day or so behind schedule, and at the rate we were going, we were going to be finished early anyway."

The news of this was a great relief to the young entrepreneur. Considering it was already after dark and the men had just had a harrowing experience, Jedidiah told everyone to call it quits for the day and to start back first thing in the morning.

Jedidiah Davenport and Matthew Colton mounted their horses and rode towards Jedidiah's house. Phineas Hargroves climbed into the buggy he had borrowed from Jedidiah and followed behind them.

After having a hearty meal, Jedidiah and Matthew walked outside and sat on the front porch to talk. Jedidiah filled him in about the meeting at the freight office.

"Sounds like they had a lot of good ideas!" Matthew exclaimed.

"They're only temporary solutions," Jedidiah mused, his gaze drifting to the horizon where the dark outlines of his land stretched out. "I'm afraid until we can find a way to end this war with the railroad, nothing will truly be resolved."

Matthew nodded, leaning forward. "There has to be some reason Elijah Perkins is so determined to buy your land. That other property is a far better option. It's shorter, more direct, and less hills to be cleared."

Jedidiah's eyes narrowed in thought, his mind racing through the possibilities. "They're definitely up to something," he agreed, his voice tinged with determination. "But for now, our focus has to be on what we can control."

He leaned back, the weight of the challenges they faced pressing down on him. "This airship... it's more than just a project to me. It's a statement, a stand against those trying to bulldoze their way through our lives."

Matthew watched his friend, noting the resolve etched in Jedidiah's features. "You've always been one to take the bull by the horns, Jed. If anyone can steer us through this, it's you."

Jedidiah let out a soft chuckle, but his eyes held a serious glint. "Sometimes, I wonder if I'm up to the task. But then, I look at what I've built, what I'm fighting for... and I know I can't back down."

The conversation lapsed into silence, both men lost in their thoughts. Jedidiah's mind wandered. He thought of his workers, their families depending on him, and the legacy of his father's business. "This isn't just about me or the Davenport name," he thought. "It's about all of us, standing together against the tide."

As the night deepened, Jedidiah felt a renewed sense of purpose solidify within him. No matter what Perkins threw their way, he would stand firm. He was the captain of this ship, steering it through uncharted waters, determined to find a safe harbor for everyone who had placed their trust in him.

****

Despite all his previous troubles, the remainder of the week brought on a new sense of purpose. The next few weeks after that went by pretty uneventful as well. This allowed Jedidiah time to focus all of his attention on the construction of the airship. Under Jedidiah and Phineas' leadership, the crew united in a shared resolve, their spirits undimmed by the setback. The air was filled with the sounds of vigorous activity as they cleared the debris, their movements a clear sign of determination and strength.

Jedidiah stood amongst his men, his voice ringing clear and confident as he addressed them. "This airship is more than just a vessel. It's a testament to our resilience!" The men nodded, their faces set with a renewed vigor, as they turned their hands to the task of rebuilding.

In no time, the damaged section of the airship began to take shape once more, its framework being pieced together with meticulous care. The progress was tangible.

The second week brought its share of challenges - unexpected thunderstorms, and technical difficulties in the airship's design. Yet, each hurdle was met with Phineas' characteristic ingenuity and the crew's unwavering dedication.

One afternoon, as a particularly intricate part of the airship posed a problem, Phineas, with a twinkle in his eye, unveiled a clever solution that left the crew both baffled and impressed. Jedidiah watched with a mix of admiration and amusement, as the eccentric inventor demonstrated his workaround, his hands moving with the precision of a maestro.

During this week, Jedidiah and Jim found themselves working closely on the installation of the airship's propulsion system. The camaraderie between them was evident, yet Jedidiah's gaze would occasionally linger on Jim, a silent echo of his unresolved suspicions.

As the third and final week arrived, a sense of anticipation hung over the ranch. The airship, now almost complete, stood reaching the very top of the hangar it had been constructed in. The engines had been tested and were purring smoothly, and the navigation instruments were being calibrated.

The excitement was contagious, everyone's conversations filled with talk of the upcoming maiden voyage. Phineas, ever the perfectionist, was seen flitting from one end of the airship to the other, ensuring every detail was up to his exacting standards.

One evening, as the sun dipped below the horizon, casting long shadows across the land, Jedidiah climbed up on the roof of the building. Alone with his thoughts, he looked out over the expanse of his ranch, reflecting on the journey that had brought him here. The challenges, the triumphs, the unyielding spirit of his crew - it was all embodied in the vessel before him.

As the final preparations for the airship's maiden voyage were being made, Phineas B. Hargroves approached Jedidiah Davenport with a question that had been lingering in his mind. His curious gaze fixed on the young entrepreneur, Phineas inquired, "Jedidiah, now that the moment of truth is upon us, I must ask you once again - how do you plan to power the opening and closing of this massive roof?"

Jedidiah's eyes sparkled with a hint of mystery and excitement. "Ah, Phineas, I've been waiting to show you this," he said, leading the inventor to a corner of the expansive building. A dusty tarp sat covering an oddly shaped object whose purpose had not yet been revealed.

With a flourish, Jedidiah pulled off the cover, unveiling a small but intricate steam-powered engine. The machine, compact and robust, was a marvel of engineering, its pipes and gears gleaming under the soft light filtering through the barn.

"This," the young inventor announced proudly, "is a compact steam engine that I designed and built months ago. It wasn't originally intended for this, but it suits our needs perfectly."

Phineas' eyes widened in amazement as he examined the engine. "My dear boy, this is ingenious!" he exclaimed, his voice tinged with admiration and a hint of envy.

Jedidiah smiled, a sense of pride swelling in his chest. "It's compact and powerful, ideal for controlling the roof mechanism."

As Phineas continued to inspect the engine, Jedidiah explained its workings. "You see, once started, it generates enough power to move the gears connected to the roof. It's efficient and reliable – exactly what we need for tomorrow's launch."

Phineas nodded, his mind already racing with possibilities. "Remarkable, Jedidiah. This small engine not only solves our immediate problem but opens doors for future innovations."

The two men spent the next hour discussing the engine's capabilities, modifications, and potential applications. Phineas, ever the inventor, was brimming with ideas on how to enhance and adapt the design.

"But we can continue to discuss plans for improving this engine another time. We need to get some rest because tomorrow, we take to the skies!" Jedidiah exclaimed, triumphantly.

****

The next morning, as the sun began to rise, casting a warm glow over the ranch, the sound of the steam engine chugging to life filled the air. The roof of the hangar, a colossal structure of wood and metal, began to open slowly and smoothly, revealing the vast expanse of the morning sky.

Pat Bennington, Agatha Porter, Jim Davis, and all the ranch hands gathered around in the open field. The airship, with Jedidiah Davenport, Matthew Colton, and Phineas B. Hargroves aboard began to float effortlessly into the air. It was now fully visible for all to see. Phineas instructed Jedidiah on how to maneuver the craft and set it down almost directly next to his own airship, the Icarus.

After landing it, Davenport opened the door and lowered the ramp. He invited everyone aboard for a tour. Jedidiah and Phineas stood next to each other, their eyes beaming with pride as they conducted a small impromptu ceremony.

Matthew stepped forward, handing Jedidiah a bottle of wine. "Time to make it official, Jed."

"Christen it?" Jedidiah asked confused.

"Of course, my dear boy," Phineas spoke up in agreement. "It wouldn't be proper to launch a ship on its maiden voyage without christening it!"

"What are you going to call it?" Matthew asked, his eyes practically dancing with excitement.

The crowd gathered around, their faces lit with anticipation. Among them, Jim Davis stood a bit apart, his expression one of quiet pride. His eyes met Jedidiah's, and for a moment, the unresolved questions between them were suspended.

"Call it?" Jedidiah suddenly realized this was one thing he hadn't given much thought to.

"Surely you've thought about it, a little?" Phineas asked.

"It sure is a sleek-looking craft!" Pat Bennington spoke up. "I bet it'll even outrun Hargrove's ship!"

"Well they are almost identical in every aspect," Phineas spoke up a little defensive of his personal vessel. "I did use the same design specs for both. Although, I will admit that I threw in some tweaks and improvements on Jedidiah's craft."

"How about you call it, The Swift?" Jim Davis chimed in.

"The Swift," Jedidiah echoed, pondering for a moment. "I do like the sound of that for an airship.

I may just use that one for a later one. After all, if things go as planned this won't be the last ship I sail into the air!"

"Well for Pete's sake!" Agatha Porter blurted out. "What are you going to call it?"

"This airship represents a lot more than just a way to travel and transport goods," Jedidiah reflected, pausing for a moment to consider the journey that brought them to this point. "It wasn't even a month ago that most of us were inside that very building, fighting to put out a raging fire. Some thought that would be the end of the ranch."

He looked around at the faces of those gathered, their expressions a mix of anticipation and pride. "We've had a lot of obstacles to overcome," he continued. "But we rose from the ashes, both literally and metaphorically."

Taking a dramatic pause, he held the moment, allowing the significance to sink in. Then, with a confident nod, he declared, "I know what I'm going to call this ship. I christen this vessel, the Phoenix!"

The crowd erupted into cheers as Jedidiah swung the bottle of wine and smashed it against the hull of the airship. Champagne sprayed in a sparkling arc, catching the early rays of the morning sun.

"Here's to 'the Phoenix' and her maiden voyage!" Phineas shouted, his voice full of emotion.

Matthew laughed, clapping Jedidiah on the back. "Couldn't have chosen a better name myself."

Pat Bennington, wiping a tear from his eye, remarked, "It's a beauty, Jed. Truly a sight to behold."

Jedidiah nodded, his gaze sweeping over the crowd, over the faces of those who had become not just workers or acquaintances but friends and companions in this incredible journey.

Amongst the excitement, Jedidiah glanced at the label still attached to what was left of the bottle, looked at Matthew, and said, "This was a pretty expensive bottle of champagne. You didn't have to spend this much money on it."

"I didn't..." Matthew replied simply, "I charged it to your account."

As Jedidiah was about to respond, Pat Bennington spoke up and said, "Hey Jed, before I forget, I picked up this package for you the other day when I went into town for supplies." He handed over a small box wrapped in brown paper and tied with twine. It had Jedidiah's name on it and underneath that, it said, Davenport Ranch.

"The other day?" Jedidiah asked confused, as he took the package from his portly cook. "Why are you just now giving it to me?"

"Well, the fellow who handed it to me asked me to be sure not to give it to you until the day you finished building your airship!"

Jedidiah and Matthew exchanged a knowing glance.

"I'm not sure I like the sounds of that!" Matthew exclaimed.

"Neither do I!" Jedidiah agreed as he held the package up in front of him. He began to examine it more closely.

"Are you going to open it or not, Jed?" Pat asked, excitedly. "I can't wait to see what it is!"

With nimble fingers, Jedidiah cautiously untied the twine and peeled back the paper. The room seemed to hold its breath as he lifted the lid, revealing a silver pocket watch with a gold-embossed train on the front.

A hushed silence fell over the group as Jedidiah read the note inside the lid, "You think your dream's about to take flight but think again. Your time is running out!"

A hushed silence fell over the group as
Jedidiah read the note inside the lid.

CHAPTER XIII

The Celebration

"Your time is running out!" Jedidiah Davenport's voice echoed across the deck of his airship.

Matthew stepped closer, his brow furrowed, showing great concern. "This is no joke, Jed," he said. "They really mean business this time!"

Phineas, ever the optimist, clapped his hands together. "Pish-posh! Empty threats from a man who's losing his grip on reality. This Perkins fellow is grasping at straws."

Jim Davis, who had remained silent up until now, stepped forward, his eyes narrowed in thought. "We need to be cautious. This isn't something to take lightly, Jed."

Jedidiah nodded, his gaze shifting between the note and the watch. The message was clear. It was a direct threat from Perkins.

He placed the items back in the box and with a

look of determination, said, "We've faced challenges before, and we'll face this one. Perkins wants to intimidate me, but I won't back down. Not now, not ever."

The group nodded in agreement, their faces a mix of concern and resolve. They stood united, a testament to the bond they had formed in the face of adversity.

Jedidiah Davenport lingered for a moment, staring at the box. Suddenly, he looked around at the crowd of people working for him and reminded himself that this was a party. "Don't just stand there!" he said. "We've just finished building an airship! Let's celebrate!"

Jedidiah's call for celebration began to lift the mood. The realization of their achievement slowly replaced their recent anxiety, as the morning sun shone brightly on the deck of the Phoenix, and the party commenced.

Pat Bennington, with his usual jovial demeanor, emerged from the lower deck, his arms full of trays of refreshments. "Let's not let a bit of bad news spoil our day!" he boomed, his voice carrying over the deck. "We've got an airship to celebrate!"

Agatha Porter followed suit, her skilled hands balancing a large jug of freshly squeezed lemonade. Despite her usually stern demeanor, a smile graced her face as she set down her burden. "Drink up, everyone. You'll need your strength for all the celebrating!"

Everyone immediately began to gather around the makeshift buffet. Amongst other things, there were homemade biscuits, a selection of cured meats, and an array of cheeses. Each dish was carefully prepared by Pat and Agatha. It was a feast fit for a king.

As Matthew Colton leaned against the railing, he took a bite of one of the biscuits and grinned at Jedidiah. "Pat's outdone himself again," he commented as he brushed a few crumbs from his shirt.

Jedidiah, standing amidst his friends and hired hands, allowed himself a moment to breathe. The worries about Perkins and the mysterious package temporarily vanished as he watched everyone come together, their faces brightening with laughter.

Phineas, always the eccentric, had a group of wide-eyed ranch hands captivated with tales of his past inventions, each more fantastical than the last. Jim Davis, typically more reserved, relaxed a bit and visibly became more comfortable as he joined in on the conversations, occasionally throwing in bits of dry humor.

As the celebration continued, Jedidiah's gaze wandered to the horizon, where the vast expanse of his ranch lay. He knew the challenges ahead would be daunting, but the sense of unity and friendship on the deck of the Phoenix gave him hope.

In the warmth of the morning sun, with the sounds of laughter and lively conversations all around him, Jedidiah raised his glass in a silent toast to the future, to determination, and to the unwavering spirit of the people who had become more than just hired hands.

"Okay, so who's up for a free trip in an airship?" Jedidiah called out anxious to start on their maiden voyage. "Agatha? Pat?"

"You wouldn't catch me floating around the sky in one of these things!" Agatha Porter exclaimed, with a look of determination.

Pat nodded his head as he agreed with the older woman. "I'm afraid I'd rather have both of my feet planted firmly on the ground myself. I'm too old to be traipsing off towards the stars!"

Jedidiah turned to his foreman and asked if he or any of his men would like to go.

"Jed, do you really think we should go off and leave the ranch unguarded?" Jim Davis asked in response. "As it is, we've had almost every available person working on this project for the past month and I'm afraid to leave the range unprotected any longer."

Jedidiah thought about this for a moment and then agreed with his foreman. "Of course, you're right. I just got caught up in the moment." Turning towards Matthew Colton and Phineas B. Hargroves, he said, "Guess it's just the three of us!"

"Perhaps it's for the best, my dear boy," Phineas placed a reassuring hand on the younger man's shoulder. "We wouldn't want to place anyone else's lives at risk on our trial voyage."

"Yeah, Jed, we wouldn't want to put anyone else's lives at..." Matthew was echoing the eccentric man's words when he suddenly cut his sentence short and whirled his head around with a look of shock on his face. "What do you mean, lives at risk?"

"Oh, think nothing of it, my dear boy," Phineas chuckled. "There's always a certain amount of risk involved when testing something out for the first time. If I thought there was any real chance of danger involved, I wouldn't be going along myself

The word danger made Jedidiah's mind suddenly race back to the incident a few weeks ago when a section of the ship collapsed during the early build stages. "Did you ever find out what caused the timbers to collapse?" he asked Phineas.

"Timbers to collapse?" Hargroves asked confused.

Slightly annoyed that Phineas had taken the incident so lightly that he had completely forgotten about it, Jedidiah took a deep breath and said, "When part of the airship collapsed and pinned you under it..."

"Oh yes!" The eccentric older man replied. "It seems that whoever had nailed together the supports used the wrong nails. They weren't long enough and pulled loose under the extreme weight."

"And are we sure that only the correct size nails were used after that?"

"My dear boy, I give you my word that I personally inspected every section of this vessel as it was being assembled!"

Jedidiah nodded, processing Phineas' words. Despite the reassurance, a hint of concern lingered in his mind about the ship's safety, but he chose to trust in Phineas' expertise and diligence. Shifting his focus to the journey ahead, he turned to address the gathered crowd with renewed determination.

Jedidiah once again thanked everyone for their hard work and dedication. He ended his speech by saying, "We would love to stay here and continue celebrating with you, but we need to get started on our voyage!"

One by one everyone who passed by, congratulated and wished the three men luck on their trip. After the last person had stepped off, Jedidiah pulled up the ramp and closed the door.

After only the three of them remained, the mood shifted as they began the final preparations for the maiden voyage. The Phoenix stood tall and imposing, its structure casting a long shadow across the field, with its sister ship, the Icarus, only a few feet away.

Matthew Colton looked to his friend, his excitement mingled with a touch of nervousness. "We're ready to go, Jed," he called out, trying to sound more confident than he felt.

Jedidiah turned to Matthew, a determined look on his face. "Let's do one final walk-through, just to be sure," he replied. The seriousness in his voice underscored the gravity of the moment.

Together they walked along the deck, checking every detail with meticulous care. Their eyes scanned the gauges, the ropes, and the pulleys, ensuring everything was in perfect order.

Phineas Hargroves, also conducting a final inspection, double-checked the navigation instruments and the airship's propulsion system. His usual eccentricity was replaced by a focused intensity, indicative of the importance of the task at hand.

As they completed their inspection, the three of them gathered around the helm, their faces reflecting a mix of emotions: pride in their work, anticipation for the voyage, and a hint of apprehension about what lay ahead.

The heart of the Phoenix, its engine, was a marvel of engineering. Intricate brass pipes intertwined with valves emanating soft hisses of steam, a symphony of mechanical life.

The engine's rhythmic chugging was a promising melody to their ears, resonating with the promise of adventure. Its exterior, a tapestry of polished wood panels and ornate copper fittings, gleamed in the morning light, reflecting the careful craftsmanship that had gone into its creation.

The interior of the airship blended Victorian elegance with futuristic functionality. The control deck was a testament to this fusion: brass levers and gauges with detailed engravings sat alongside advanced navigation instruments.

A traditional compass, encased within a network of gears and cogs, sat next to a table covered in maps and charts.

In the corner stood a unique communication device, resembling an old-fashioned brass tube intercom, modified to send Morse code messages throughout the airship.

Safety features were not overlooked, with steam-powered fire suppression systems and a mechanical arm for mid-flight repairs, showcasing both innovation and practicality.

Jedidiah, Matthew, and Phineas were dressed appropriately for the occasion. Their outfits were a nod to the era of exploration and invention, featuring leather vests adorned with brass buttons, and utility belts holding an array of brass tools and gadgets. Jedidiah had been wearing a coat for the celebration, but he had taken it off to start their journey.

The helm itself was a work of art, inlaid with

ivory and ebony, its smooth surface inviting to the touch. Above them, the canopy of the airship housed the innovative propulsion system. Harnessing the power of steam with ingenuity, it promised a journey as thrilling as it was efficient.

Jim Davis, who had been quietly observing the preparations from the ground, called out, "Everything looks good, Jed!" He offered a supportive nod. His presence, a constant source of strength, added to the growing confidence among the three men.

"Alright then," Jedidiah said, clapping his hands together. "Let's get this beauty into the air."

"Jedidiah, wait!" Phineas cleared his throat as he reached under the control panel and picked up a beautifully crafted wooden box. He had hidden it under there the night before. He opened the lid and retrieved a brand new cap, its fabric rich and durable. The top was rounded and there was a pair of intricately designed goggles resting on the small stiff brim.

"For you, Captain Davenport," Phineas said with a flourish. "A hat befitting a man of your stature and goggles for the skies you're about to conquer. These are no ordinary goggles. They're equipped with multiple lenses. They'll serve you well at various altitudes."

Jedidiah accepted the gifts, a smile spreading across his face as he placed the cap on his head and

He opened the lid and retrieved a brand new cap, its fabric rich and durable. The top was rounded and there was a pair of intricately designed goggles resting on the small stiff brim.

examined the goggles. "They're perfect, Phineas. Thank you."

Turning to Matthew, Phineas presented a similar box. "And for you, Mr. Colton, to ensure you're equally equipped for our journey."

Matthew's eyes widened in surprise as he received his own set of gear. "I didn't expect this... Thank you!"

"How did you manage to go out and buy these things?" Jedidiah asked as he replaced the goggles on the brim of his cap.

Phineas Hargroves merely smiled as he said, "My dear boy, these are extras I had lying around the cabin of my own ship. It always pays to be prepared!" The older man became more serious as he said, "Now let's get this craft of yours in the air!"

With that said, Matthew, Phineas, and Jedidiah took their positions. The engine hummed to life, its rhythmic chugging a promising melody to their ears. The workers on the ground surrounding the vessel stepped back, their eyes fixed on the Phoenix as it began to lift off the ground, graceful and majestic.

As the airship ascended, a cheer erupted from the onlookers. Jedidiah looked out from the deck, his heart swelling with pride.

The Phoenix soared higher, its shadow diminishing as it climbed towards the open sky.

This ascent marked the beginning of an extraordinary journey for Jedidiah Davenport, Matthew Colton, and Phineas B. Hargroves.

As the ranch below them and the people cheering them continued to grow increasingly smaller, Phineas turned to Jedidiah and asked him where he planned to take them.

"Where?" The young entrepreneur asked, slightly confused. "I just thought we'd take it around the ranch maybe over Spoon Fork and back again."

"That's no fun!" Matthew scoffed. "Jed, this is the maiden voyage of your very own airship. You gotta make this trip count!"

Thinking about it for a moment, Jedidiah Davenport grinned mischievously and replied, "I know the perfect place!"

"Care to share the destination with the rest of us?" Phineas asked curiously. "I can at least enter the coordinates into your navigation system."

Jedidiah stood up straight and with a look of mystery said, "Mr. Hargroves, prepare to enter the following coordinates: Second star to the right and straight on till morning!" His words hung in the air, charged with excitement and possibility.

CHAPTER XIV

The Maiden Voyage

The Phoenix, sailing high and soaring majestically through the clouds, carried Jedidiah, Matthew, and Phineas into a realm where the vast fields below them sprawled like a patchwork quilt. The sun, a radiant orb in the clear sky, cast a warm glow over the deck where the three men stood, each absorbed in his thoughts.

Jedidiah, at the helm, felt a surge of exhilaration. He steered the airship purposefully, its engines humming a steady, rhythmic song of progress and hope.

Below them, the world seemed like a different place. The troubles that tethered them to the earth appeared smaller, and more manageable from this new vantage point. As they glided over the valley, heads turned upwards, eyes wide with wonder at the sight of the Phoenix.

In less than an hour, it began to dawn on

Matthew where Jedidiah was taking them. They were flying high over Hawthorne Grove and headed directly towards the temporary headquarters of the D.&R.W. Railroad.

Matthew turned to his friend and asked, "So is this what you've been so secretive about?"

Jedidiah smiled and shrugged his shoulders. "I just want Elijah Perkins to see for himself that I'm not licked yet!"

"Well, my dear boy, it looks like you're about to get your wish." Phineas B. Hargroves pointed over the side of the airship towards the railroad headquarters, where a figure had emerged onto a balcony. It was Elijah Perkins, unmistakable in his stature, his posture radiating authority and calculation. He stood there, a cigar smoldering between his fingers, his gaze locked onto the Phoenix. Even from this height, his stare felt piercing, laden with unspoken thoughts and plans.

Davenport's grip on the wheel tightened. This was the man who threatened his dream, his legacy. Yet, up here, amongst the clouds, Jedidiah felt a sense of power, a belief that he could take on whatever challenges Perkins threw his way.

For the next thirty minutes, Jedidiah hovered and flew in a circular pattern around the railroad's office buildings. This was an act of defiance and a show of strength. With his goggles in place, Jedidiah kept a watchful eye over his adversary.

"My dear boy," Phineas began to speak with an air of caution, "Do you think this is wise? After all, we don't want to provoke any more of his wrath."

Jedidiah furrowed his brow and, with determination, declared, "This man has been tormenting me for months. I want him to see what it feels like to be stalked for a change!"

At this point, Elijah Perkins retreated inside. Minutes later, he was seen sitting in the back of a black buggy as he was being driven away by one of his workers.

"I wonder where he's going," Jedidiah mused as he replaced his goggles on the brim of his hat.

"I hope he's not off to do more damage to your ranch or freight business," Matthew remarked solemnly, as he and Phineas also removed their goggles. "Jed, I think Phineas was right. This was a bad idea coming here."

"Maybe so," Jedidiah turned his back to his friends and faced the direction his adversary was riding in. "I just wanted him to see I'm not backing down, and I'm prepared to bring the fight to him!"

"Well," Phineas Hargroves laughed, "You've definitely let your presence be known!"

Jedidiah returned to the helm and asked, "Where to now?" His countenance changed completely to one of a carefree attitude. "This is the maiden voyage of the Phoenix, the greatest airship to ever sail the skies!"

Mr. Hargroves suddenly cleared his throat as a clear reminder that he too had an airship. "One of the greatest, my dear boy, one of the greatest!"

Jedidiah's face broke into a wide grin, as he said, "Not counting the Icarus, of course!"

"That's more like it!" Phineas stated with pride. Despite designing both his ship and Jedidiah's, he was the most proud of his own vessel. Even though airships had already been around for almost thirty years at the time he built the Icarus, his ship was unique. It was his design, with his own special tweaks and enhancements.

"Okay," Jedidiah became focused again. "Let's not forget what we're doing. Does anyone have any place they'd like to see or visit while we're testing out the Phoenix?"

Matthew began to smile from ear to ear and said, "Actually, I have a suggestion!" Matthew's eyes sparkled with an adventurous glint. "Gentlemen, how about we take the Phoenix over the Spoon Fork Canyon? I bet it's something to see from above!"

Jedidiah nodded in agreement, his face lighting up at the prospect of exploring the majestic canyon from the skies. "To Spoon Fork Canyon it is. Let's see what the Phoenix is truly capable of."

As they adjusted their course, the landscape below them transitioned. The green expanse of the plains gradually giving way to the rugged, awe-inspiring beauty of Spoon Fork Canyon. The Phoenix glided gracefully, its shadow a fleeting wisp over the jagged cliffs and winding river below.

Phineas leaned over the railing, his gaze fixed on the canyon's depths. "Remarkable, isn't it? The world is full of such wonders, and we're among the few who get to see it from this vantage point."

"It certainly is!" Jedidiah agreed as he stepped away from the helm to enjoy the view as well.

The noonday sun hung high in the sky as the Phoenix continued its graceful arc over Spoon Fork Canyon. The beauty of the scene was not lost on Jedidiah and his companions, each immersed in their own thoughts amid the tranquility of the flight, with ample time ahead for further exploration.

Jedidiah drifted back to the ranch and the looming threat of Perkins. The joy of exploration was tinged with the weight of responsibility and the battles yet to come.

Matthew, breaking the silence, turned to Jedidiah with a curious sparkle in his eye. "Jed, why don't we fly over the old mining town? It's been abandoned for years, but from up here, it might just give us a new perspective."

Jedidiah nodded, his eyes reflecting a blend of excitement and nostalgia. "The old mining town, eh? Sounds like a plan." Adjusting the controls, he

The Phoenix glided gracefully, its shadow
a fleeting wisp over the jagged cliffs and
winding river below.

gently guided the Phoenix towards their new destination.

"Hey Jed, remember the time when we were kids and we got trapped in the mine shaft?" Matthew smiled as the thought came to him. His eyes gleamed with the mischief of a memory well cherished.

Jedidiah smiled, his eyes crinkling with amusement. "How could I forget? We had just turned thirteen. We were full of curiosity and too much daring for our own good."

"That summer was something else," Matthew added, his voice tinged with nostalgia. "We thought we were invincible, exploring every nook and cranny of the old town. But that abandoned mine was our real test."

****

Nearly fifteen years earlier, two boys known as Jedidiah Davenport and Matthew Colton stood before a gaping mouth of darkness, which was the entrance to Spoon Fork mine. Both boys on the cusp of adolescence, armed with nothing but lanterns and a shared sense of invincibility, dared to venture inside.

"Are you sure about this, Jed?" Matthew asked nervously, as they stepped into the cool, musty air of the mine.

"Scared, Matty?" Jedidiah, ever the leader, flashed a grin. "Don't be. It's just an old mine."

The beams of their lanterns cut through the darkness, casting long, dancing shadows. They ventured deeper, laughing and just enjoying the adventure.

"Hey, Matthew!" Jedidiah called out to his friend to show him a rock formation. He was taken a bit off guard as he heard his voice suddenly echoing off every wall.

Matthew turned around, his eyes beaming with excitement, he asked, "How'd you do that?" His voice also echoed back at him.

Both boys burst into laughter, turning their echoes into a contest to see who could be the loudest. This went on for several minutes until a sudden rumble silenced them. All of a sudden, the world came crashing down around them!

The dust settled, revealing their new reality. They were trapped. The way they had come in was blocked by fallen timber and rock. Panic stricken, both boys began to claw at the debris trying in vain to clear the path. After about twenty minutes, they realized it was fruitless.

"What are we gonna do now?" Matthew asked as he wearily plopped down on a nearby rock.

Jedidiah picked up one of the two still-lit lanterns, moving it to the side so he could sit down as well. "This can't be the only way in or out!" he declared.

"You think we can find another way?" Matthew suddenly sat up on the edge of his rock, with a new sense of purpose.

"We've got to try. What other choice do we have?" Jedidiah asked as he stood up and started walking down the tunnel.

The two young boys explored the depths of the mine well into the night, trying to find a way out. Finally, too exhausted to go any further, and with their lanterns about to go out, they found a spot to lay down and rest.

After a restless sleep in the old mine, unsure if they'd ever get out, they were woken by a shaft of light coming from the end of the tunnel. Matthew was the first one to wake. He turned and shook his friend until he too was awake. They both stood up and ran towards the light until they emerged above ground. Both started screaming with joy as they took in deep breaths of fresh air.

****

Jedidiah nodded, his eyes returning to the present. "Those were the days, my friend. We've come a long way since then. But some lessons stay with you forever."

As the memory faded, the bonds of their childhood adventure seemed to strengthen their resolve for the challenges ahead. The Phoenix continued its journey, carrying not just the men they were now but also the echoes of the boys they once were.

As they neared the ghostly outlines of the abandoned buildings, the contrast between the past and present was stark. The skeletal remains of the once-thriving mining community lay silent below them, a testament to the relentless march of time.

"It's incredible," Phineas murmured, his eyes tracing the contours of the deserted streets and broken structures. "To think life was once bustling down there, and now..." the older man cut his sentence short as he placed his goggles over his eyes. "Say, who are those men down there?"

"That's Leroy Johnson and his gang of outlaws!" Matthew exclaimed.

"What are they doing here?" Jedidiah asked as he lowered his own goggles, observing them entering the same mine shaft from his and Matthew's youth. "I don't think they've noticed us..." Turning back to Phineas, he said, "Take the wheel and land us on the hill behind the mine."

"Are we going to go find out what they're up to?" Matthew asked, as he drew his gun from his side and made sure it was loaded.

Jedidiah noticed the weapon in his friend's hand and said, 'Hopefully, we won't need that. However...'" He went into the cabin that would be used as his sleeping quarters for long journeys and returned with another of his rifles, equipped with a special long-range scope

After Phineas skillfully landed the Phoenix, Jedidiah opened the door and lowered the ramp. Jedidiah and Matthew descended and made their way down the hill. Cautiously, they approached the mine shaft entrance, their memories racing back to that day nearly fifteen years ago.

"It looks like they've cleared out the collapsed portion of the tunnel!" Jedidiah remarked as he peeked his head inside.

Matthew glanced around and spotted a pile of rock and dirt nearby. "I think you're right. This must be from inside!"

"Get back!" Suddenly, Jedidiah pulled his head away from the entrance, turning towards his friend and shoving him to the ground.

"Argh!!!" Matthew groaned as he was hit in a flying tackle. But he was immediately glad he had been, as he heard the sounds of hoofbeats and witnessed the sight of four armed men galloping out of the tunnel. It was Leroy Johnson and the three men who had tried to bully Jedidiah weeks ago in Spoon Fork.

Both men on the ground breathed a sigh of relief as they watched them ride out of sight. None of them looked back or noticed as they went galloping by.

"What do you suppose they were doing in there?" Matthew asked, as he stood to his feet and began dusting off his clothes.

"Maybe they've been doing some prospecting?" Jedidiah shrugged his shoulders as he, too, stood up and dusted himself off. "I'm gonna go inside and find out!"

Matthew reluctantly followed behind, both of them painfully aware of what happened the last time they entered this mine shaft. This time, they didn't need any lanterns as there were ones already lit and attached to new timbers supporting the walls and ceiling of the mine.

"I don't think they're mining this place..." Jedidiah pointed towards bedrolls and other supplies. In the middle of this was the remains of a campfire. "I think they've been using this place as a hideout."

"Well, they're welcome to it!" Matthew exclaimed. "I never want to spend another night down here again."

Jedidiah agreed, and the two turned and exited the mine. After climbing back up the hill, they re-boarded the airship and started their return flight home.

****

Night had already begun to settle as they floated

over the ranch. Despite this, they immediately noticed unusual activity below them. Several carriages were parked outside the Davenport estate. This was an uncommon sight, especially at this hour.

With a look of confusion, Jedidiah glanced at the other two men and asked, "What's going on?"

Putting on his goggles, Matthew looked over the side and said, "I don't know but I have a bad feeling about it!"

"Perhaps, my dear boy, you should try landing here instead of in the barn," Phineas suggested. "That way, we can quickly find out what's happening. I can take it back up and store it in the hangar for you."

Jedidiah nodded and effortlessly landed the Phoenix about a hundred feet from his house. He and Matthew quickly disembarked, their minds racing with possibilities. The unexpected visitors at this hour could only mean something significant, potentially troubling, was afoot.

They approached the main house with a sense of urgency. The front door swung open, revealing Sheriff Thompson, his two deputies Eli Carter and Wesley Holt, as well as Mr. Simmons from the Spoon Fork bank.

Jedidiah's brow furrowed as he glanced back and forth at the visitors and asked, "What's going on here?"

"Jed, I just wanted you to know I had nothing to do with this..." Mr. Simmons looked down to the floor too ashamed to look at Jedidiah in the face.

Becoming both anxious and outraged, Jedidiah demanded, "Do with what?"

"Jed, I wouldn't be here if the law didn't say I had to be," Sheriff Thompson said reluctantly.

Almost at the point of screaming, Jedidiah took a deep breath and asked, "Would someone just please tell me what's going on?"

Sheriff Thompson replied by handing him a folded document and saying, "Maybe you should just read it for yourself."

Unfolding the paper and reading it, Jedidiah gasped, "Elijah Perkins has purchased my loan from the bank and is foreclosing on the ranch!"

CHAPTER XV

Shadows of Betrayal

"Perkins bought the loan and now he's foreclosing!" Jedidiah's voice trembled, a mix of disbelief and anger evident in his tone.

"Foreclosing!" Pat Bennington exclaimed. He stood a few feet away in the doorway to the kitchen. A resounding gasp echoed from Agatha Porter, standing next to him.

"How long do you have?" she asked, her voice filled with a mix of worry and dread.

Jedidiah glanced up from the paper and replied, "One week..."

"One week!" she exclaimed.

Matthew paced the room, his fists clenched. "How could he do this? There must be some way to fight it!"

Sheriff Thompson nodded solemnly, his expression one of regret. "I'm sorry, Jed. Like I said, I wouldn't be here if it weren't absolutely necessary. The law requires..."

Jedidiah cut him off, his gaze hardening. "The law? Perkins is using the law to steal my ranch!"

Mr. Simmons, the banker, finally spoke up, his voice laced with guilt. "I tried to delay it, Jed, but Perkins... he's powerful. I couldn't stop it."

Jedidiah, clenching the foreclosure notice, looked around at the faces of his friends and allies. The gravity of the situation was settling in. Each one was aware of the monumental challenge they now faced. The fight for the Davenport ranch was just beginning.

"How did Elijah Perkins even know that I took out the loan on the ranch?" He once again looked to the others for answers, but nobody had one. Some of them standing there didn't even know about the loan until that very moment.

"What are you going to do now, Jed?" Pat Bennington asked, breaking the tension. "How are you going to get out of this one?"

"I might know a way," Mr. Simmons spoke up. "It's not the best option, but you could downsize your freight company and sell off some of your assets."

"That would put me out of business!" Jedidiah protested. "So basically, I'm at a point where I have to choose: Do I want to save my ranch or the company that I built from the ground up?"

"It won't come to that, Jed," Agatha Porter

stated in a nurturing manner, which was unlike her usual demeanor. "You'll figure a way out of this. You always do!"

While this was happening, unbeknownst to everyone in the room, a dark figure lurked a few feet away outside the entrance door, listening to the entire conversation.

As he turned to walk away, the moonlight shone on his face, revealing the features of Jim Davis.

****

The next morning, Jedidiah got up before anyone else and decided to take a trip to the D.&R.W. Railroad and finally confront Elijah Perkins face to face. He left a note on the kitchen table stating where he had gone.

As the first light of dawn painted the sky in hues of pink and orange, Jedidiah Davenport saddled his horse, Blaze. The cool morning air was a comfort to his troubled thoughts, but the weight of the foreclosure notice lay heavy in his heart.

He set off at a steady pace, determined to confront Elijah Perkins face to face. As Blaze trotted along the familiar path to Hawthorn Grove, Jedidiah's mind raced with possible scenarios of the confrontation. He knew that Perkins was a cunning man, not easily swayed or intimidated. Yet, Jedidiah's resolve was as strong as the iron tracks that wound through the countryside.

The journey to Hawthorn Grove was a solitary one, giving Jedidiah time to reflect on everything that led to this moment.

After a few hours, he finally reached the temporary headquarters of the D.&R.W. Railroad. A two-story building stood in the center of the sprawling complex of temporary structures and bustling activity. He dismounted Blaze, tying her to a nearby post, and strode towards the main office with a firm step. His boots kicked up small clouds of dust with each movement, mirroring the storm brewing inside him.

He was almost lost among the throng of workers and officials scurrying about, papers in hand, deep in conversation. Jedidiah pushed through the swarm, his eyes searching for Perkins. With determination, he stormed upstairs to the second floor. He spotted him in a spacious office, talking animatedly to a group of well-dressed men.

Without hesitation, Jedidiah barged into the room, the door slamming against the wall with a thud that stunned everyone into silence. All eyes turned to him, but his were fixed on Perkins, who looked up, surprise quickly morphing into a sly smile

"Mr. Davenport, to what do I owe this unexpected pleasure?" Perkins' voice was smooth, dripping with false cordiality.

"I'm here about the foreclosure," Jedidiah said, his voice steady despite the anger simmering within. "I won't let you steal my ranch, Perkins!"

The railroad executive leaned back in his chair, eyeing Jedidiah with a calculating gaze. He took a deep puff of his cigar. "Steal, Mr. Davenport? Everything I've done is within the confines of the law. You defaulted on your loan, and I merely capitalized on an opportunity."

Jedidiah clenched his fists at his sides and said, "Defaulted! How? The first payment wasn't even due yet!"

Perkins stood up, his eyes cold. "Read the fine print of your agreement, Mr. Davenport. The holder of the loan, which is me, has the right to demand full payment at any given time. If you fail to produce said payment, I can foreclose."

The tension in the room was thick. Jedidiah knew arguing with Perkins was like trying to argue with a brick wall. Yet, he couldn't back down, not when so much was at stake.

"Why are you so determined to take my land?"

"You're standing in the way of progress, boy!" Perkins took another puff of his cigar. "Just think of all your friends and neighbors and how they'll benefit from the railroad coming to the valley!"

"You know my land isn't the best option for your train!" Jedidiah approached his desk and leaned over it. "You and I both know you have

Jedidiah clenched his fists at his sides.

some other reason for wanting my land and I'm gonna find out what it is!"

Perkins cleared his throat and glanced nervously around the room before saying, "I don't know what you're talking about." He suddenly took on a more confident demeanor as two armed men came into the room and grabbed Jedidiah by his shoulders, dragging him away. "Take my advice, son. Sell me the section the railroad needs, and I'll drop the foreclosure. Because, mark my words, one way or another, I will own that land!"

"Mark my words," Jedidiah stated with a conviction that hid his inner turmoil, "I'll find a way to save my ranch!" As he was dragged through the open doorway, he shouted, "This isn't over, Perkins!"

Jedidiah looked back and forth at the two men forcefully walking him down the stairs. He casually said to them, "You know I can find my way out of here just fine..." Neither, however, said a word until they had him at the front door and shoved him onto the ground.

"A piece of advice," one of the two men said, "unless you're ready to sign that bill of sale, I wouldn't come back!"

"Thanks," Jedidiah said as he stood up, dusted himself off, mounted Blaze, and gently nudged his horse to begin riding away.

Instead of going straight home or back to Spoon

Fork, Davenport decided to ride into Hawthorn Grove. He figured he might as well check on this branch of his freight line while he had the chance.

Jedidiah entered the familiar town, its comforting atmosphere greeting him like an old friend. The streets were bustling with the daily activities of the townsfolk, their friendly chatter and laughter filling the air. He steered Blaze towards the Davenport Dispatch & Delivery Company, feeling a sense of purpose amid his recent troubles.

The office, a modest but well-maintained building, stood proudly in the heart of the town. As Jedidiah dismounted, he was greeted by the sight of Clara Johnson, the office manager. Her warm smile and confident demeanor were a comfort to him.

"Jed, what brings you to Hawthorn Grove?" Clara asked, her voice tinged with concern upon noticing the serious expression on Jedidiah's face.

Davenport sighed, "Clara, I need to discuss some urgent matters." He followed her into the office, the door closing behind them with a soft click.

Inside, the room was a hive of activity, with maps of routes and schedules lining the walls. Clara offered him a seat, her attentive gaze encouraging him to speak. Jedidiah shared the news of Perkins' foreclosure and its potential impact on the company. "I may find myself in a position where I'm forced to choose between my ranch and my freight company."

Clara listened intently, her expression turning thoughtful. "You'll find a way through this, Jed. Your ranch is your home, and this company is more than just a business. It's a lifeline for the community!"

Their conversation turned to strategies and plans, with Clara's insights into the local agricultural logistics proving invaluable. As Jedidiah started to leave the office, he felt a renewed sense of determination. The support of Hawthorn Grove and Clara's unwavering loyalty reinforced his resolve to fight for his ranch and company.

As he turned to say his goodbyes, he noticed a framed photo of two young boys sitting on her desk. Thinking they each looked familiar, Jedidiah walked over and picked it up.

Clara smiled warmly, saying, "That's my son, Leroy, and his best friend, Jim."

"Davis!" Jedidiah exclaimed a look of surprise on his face.

"That's right!" Clara replied with a puzzled look. "You know Jim Davis?'

"He's the foreman at my ranch," Jedidiah simply replied as he replaced the photo on the desk. He immediately thanked Clara for her time and excused himself.

As soon as he stepped outside, Jedidiah Davenport mounted his horse, and with a look of determination, rode off at a full gallop.

****

Once he reached the ranch, Jedidiah headed straight to the bunkhouse, looking for Jim Davis. He decided the time had come to set some things straight. However, Jim was nowhere to be seen, and a ten-thousand-acre ranch was a big place to search.

Jedidiah questioned the few ranch hands he found working the range, but none of them had seen the foreman all day. Jedidiah rode over to the hangar where he stored his airship, the Phoenix. The towering figure of Phineas' ship, the Icarus, was still anchored firmly beside the building. He stepped inside and saw his own vessel undisturbed.

Jedidiah was about to give up and ride home when he heard someone walking up behind him. It was Leo Greene, the cook for the ranch hands and the very individual who had rung the alarm the night of the stampede.

"It's a beauty, Mr. Davenport!" Leo exclaimed, as he walked inside the hangar. "I hope you don't mind, I just wanted to come out and look at it while nobody was around."

Jedidiah turned to the older man and smiled,

"It's perfectly fine, Leo, and please call me, Jed."

"I wouldn't mind going up in it one day, myself!" Leo added as he walked over and ran his hand along the side of the vessel.

Jedidiah suddenly looked confused and said, "I offered to let anyone go up with me who wanted to." He furrowed his brow. "Were you not at the celebration yesterday morning?"

"Nah, can't stand crowds!"

"Well, that makes sense." Jedidiah laughed. "Leo, anytime you want to take a ride just let me know!"

"You mean it?" the older man's entire face lit up.

"I mean it!" Jedidiah nodded in affirmation. Taking on a different expression, he asked, "Leo, I don't suppose you know what part of the ranch Jim Davis is working today, do you?"

"He's not working the ranch today," Leo replied casually. "I heard him tell one of the boys that he was riding into town and wanted him to check the fences for him on the north end of the range."

"He's in town?" Jedidiah suddenly moved with urgency again. He thanked Leo Greene and ran outside, where he mounted his horse. Turning Blaze in the direction of Spoon Fork, Jedidiah once again rode off at a full gallop.

As he rode across the field in front of his house, Matthew Colton, who was sitting on his front porch, took notice. He sprang to his feet, ran to his own horse, saddled it, and headed after his friend.

When Jedidiah arrived in Spoon Fork, he went straight to the Sheriff's office. This time, he found Sheriff Thompson alone, so he was able to speak freely without anyone having to be asked to leave.

Jedidiah didn't hesitate walking in, his expression a mix of concern and determination. Sheriff Thompson, sitting behind his desk, looked up, noting the urgency in Jedidiah's eyes.

"Sheriff," Jedidiah started, "I've just learned something about Jim Davis. He and Leroy Johnson grew up together. They were childhood friends."

Thompson's eyebrows raised in astonishment. "Jim and Leroy? That would certainly explain their connection to each other."

"Do you think this means our suspicions were true?" Jedidiah asked, the weight of the question evident in his voice.

Thompson shrugged, a thoughtful look crossing his face. "It certainly doesn't look good for Davis, that's for sure."

"Do you still think I should wait before confronting him?" Jedidiah began pacing back and forth. "I was so angry when I found out. I was ready to have it out with him the moment I saw him!"

"How did you find out?" Sheriff Thompson asked curiously.

"I was at the Hawthorne Grove branch of my freight line," Jedidiah replied. "My office manager there, Clara Johnson, is none other than Leroy Johnson's mother!"

Sheriff Thompson leaned back in his chair and with a look of surprise on his face said, "Now that is unexpected!"

"I'm running out of time!" Jedidiah exploded. "Do you really expect me to keep playing the waiting game? In a week's time, I may not even have a home!"

Sheriff Thompson stood up from behind his desk and said, "No, I think it's time we bring Mr. Davis in for questioning."

As the two men stepped out onto the street, Matthew Colton came riding up at full speed. He dismounted his horse and tied it to the post in front of the Sheriff's office.

"Jed, is everything okay?" Matthew asked excitedly. "I saw you galloping by and thought it might be an emergency!"

Just as Jedidiah was about to catch his old friend up on his adventures that day, he was interrupted by the sounds of gunfire. They appeared to be coming from down the street near his freight office.

With Sheriff Thompson leading the way, Jedidiah Davenport, and Matthew Colton rushed towards the sound. As they reached the crowd gathering in the alley next to the building, they realized where the shots had come from. Forcing their way through the onlookers, Jedidiah gasped in horror at the scene before him.

Lying in the dirt, unconscious and with a bullet wound, was his friend and eccentric mentor, Phineas B. Hargroves.

Standing over him, gun in hand, was Jim Davis!

CHAPTER XVI

The Investigation

"Drop your weapon!" Sheriff Thompson shouted as he leveled his shotgun at Jim Davis. The tall, lanky foreman instinctively whirled around, prepared to shoot in defense. However, upon recognition of the lawman, he dropped his gun.

"Jim, what happened?" Jedidiah demanded his voice a blend of concern and anger.

"I... I don't know who it was, Jed," Jim stammered, his eyes wide. "But I didn't shoot him!"

Just then, the two Deputy Sheriffs, Eli Carter, and Wesley Holt, pressed through the crowd, their badges standing out as they approached to see what was going on.

"Pick up his gun and hand it to me!" Sheriff Thompson ordered his men. Eli kept Jim covered while Wesley did as instructed.

"This gun has been fired!" Sheriff Thompson declared, after a quick examination of the weapon.

"Somebody shot at us from the end of the alley!" Jim Davis stated in defense. "I was just trying to get whoever it was that shot Mr. Hargroves."

Kneeling next to the old eccentric inventor, Jedidiah checked to see if he was breathing and, with excitement in his voice, declared, "He's still alive!"

"Some of you men, carry him over to Doc Stone's office!" Sheriff Thompson shouted to the onlookers. "Jim," he looked back at the ranch hand, "I'm afraid you're gonna have to come with me!"

Matthew watched in silence, his mind racing with questions. He couldn't believe Jim would hurt Phineas or anyone else. Jedidiah was torn between his loyalty to his foreman and the scene before him.

As Phineas B. Hargroves was being carried away for medical attention, Jedidiah and Matthew followed, leaving Jim in the custody of Sheriff Thompson.

In the doctor's office, the air was thick with tension. Jedidiah and Matthew stood anxiously as Doc Stone worked meticulously over Phineas. The walls, lined with shelves of medicine bottles and medical instruments, seemed to close in around them. The only sounds were the doctor's quiet muttering and the occasional clink of metal.

"Is he gonna make it, Doc?" Jedidiah asked, with a look of concern on his face.

Doctor Stone paused, wiping his brow. "It's a touch-and-go situation," he began slowly, his voice measured. "The bullet passed clean through, which is a good sign, but there's internal bleeding. I've done what I can to stabilize him, but the next few hours are critical."

Matthew, standing at the foot of the bed, watched in solemn silence. The gravity of the situation weighed heavily on him, the reality of their predicament hitting hard.

Doctor Stone cleared his throat, breaking the heavy atmosphere. "We'll need to keep him under observation. I'll do everything in my power to ensure he pulls through."

Jedidiah nodded, his gaze not leaving Phineas. "Thank you, Doc," he murmured, the words barely audible.

As they left the doctor's office, the weight of uncertainty and the fear of losing a dear friend hung over them like a dark cloud.

Returning to the Sheriff's office, Jedidiah found Jim in a holding cell, still claiming to be innocent. "Jed, you got to believe me, I didn't shoot Phineas!" he shouted.

"Can you tell us who did?" Sheriff Thompson asked, genuinely wanting to make sure justice was served.

"I already told you, I didn't see who was shooting at us," Jim insisted, his face etched with

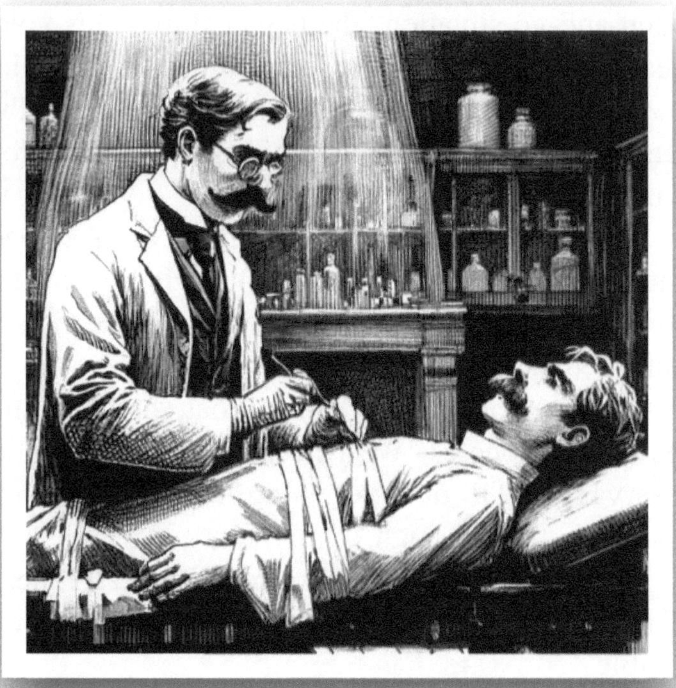

Doc Stone worked meticulously over Phineas.

desperation. "I drew my gun and fired back in self-defense!"

Sheriff Thompson interjected, "We have two witnesses who saw you ride into town right after Mr. Hargroves. They said you followed him to the freight office. Furthermore, Mr. Clayton was around back when Phineas parked his buggy. He said that he observed you ducking into the alley.

Jim Davis protested, 'I swear, I wasn't following him!' His voice carried a mix of frustration and desperation.

Sheriff Thompson, however, remained skeptical, his eyes narrowing as he scrutinized the accused. "That's hard to believe, Jim, given the circumstances," he replied coolly, his tone suggesting that he was far from convinced by Jim's assertion.

"I'll admit to arriving in town right after him," Jim Davis stated, "and heading to the freight office at the same time he did, but that's as far as it goes!"

"Why were you at the freight office? Did you plan to have another meeting with your childhood friend, Leroy Johnson?" Sheriff Thompson asked bluntly.

Jim Davis whirled his head towards the Sheriff with a look of shock on his face. "How'd you know about that?"

"I'm afraid I'm the one who told him," Jedidiah sighed as he related his trip to Hawthorn Grove and his meeting with Leroy's mother Clara Johnson.

"Okay fine," Jim dropped his gaze to the floor, then back at the Sheriff. "When I was growing up, I spent most of my time at the Johnson farm. Leroy and I were best friends. But, as we grew up, we grew apart. Leroy began associating with the wrong kind of people, and I just couldn't see myself going down that path."

"Care to explain now how your pocket watch was found in the debris after the explosion at the freight office last month?" Sheriff Thompson continued his interrogation.

"It's like I told Jed," Davis replied, defensively. "I don't know how it got in the freight office. It had been missing for several days before that ever took place."

"I'm afraid with the evidence against you," Sheriff Thompson solemnly stated, "Even if some of it may be circumstantial, I'm gonna have to hold you until the Circuit Judge comes to town."

"I didn't shoot Mr. Hargroves," Jim Davis pleaded one last time. "You've got the wrong man!"

Jedidiah's gaze lingered on Jim, torn between trust and the stark reality of the situation. The air was thick with tension as each man grappled with the weight of uncertainty hanging over them.

Matthew, who had been silently observing, finally spoke up. "Jed, I think he's telling the truth. We need to figure out what really happened.

There's more to this than meets the eye."

"I agree," Jedidiah replied affirmatively. "Like, what was Phineas doing at the freight office anyway?" He asked, with a look of puzzlement on his face.

Matthew's complexion turned white as he remembered why the older man had traveled into town. "I guess that's kind of my fault," he reluctantly explained. He shared the details about Phineas learning of the foreclosure threat and about the note Jedidiah had left before leaving that morning. "He borrowed one of your buggies and rode into town, hoping to find you!" Matthew dropped his head in shame, adding, "He heard all of it from me. If I hadn't told him, he wouldn't have come to town!"

"Well don't blame yourself," Jedidiah replied trying to comfort his friend. "He would have found out eventually. Word travels fast!"

"He's right Matt," Sheriff Thompson said agreeing.

Suddenly Jedidiah's resolve began to harden. "We can't just sit back. We need to investigate this ourselves. You know Phineas had enemies of his own. Remember the man he had the scuffle in his hotel room in Wichita?"

"Then, later, he and his partner tried to shoot us out of the sky when we were coming back!" Matthew's eyes suddenly lit up as the memory rushed back to him.

As he reached for the door handle, Jedidiah exclaimed, "Let's go see what kind of clues we can find!"

"Now hold on," Sheriff Thompson suddenly spoke up. "I don't want the two of you disturbing any evidence or interfering with our investigation!"

"Of course not, Sheriff," Jedidiah smiled, as he started out the door. "We'll just sit back and twiddle our thumbs while you figure out what really happened!"

Sheriff Thompson stared at the two men as they walked out the door, knowing full well they were going to do just the opposite of what he had said."

"We're still going to the crime scene and look for clues, aren't we?" Matthew asked the moment the door to the Sheriff's office was closed.

"I think that's obvious!" Jedidiah exclaimed as he led the way towards the freight office. "We've got to find out who did this and why. It might be our only chance to clear Jim's name and get to the bottom of this mess."

As they walked through the alley, they carefully examined every inch, looking for clues that the Sheriff might have missed. Jedidiah's keen eye caught a faint set of footprints leading away from the scene, distinct from the others.

"These footprints... they're heading towards the back of the freight office," Jedidiah noted, a sense of urgency in his voice.

Following the trail, they arrived at a small, secluded area out of the view of the wagons being loaded and unloaded. There, hidden among the shadows, they found a discarded cloth, stained with what appeared to be gunpowder.

"This could be important," Matthew said, his eyes narrowing.

"It could mean that someone else was here, someone trying to frame Jim!" Jedidiah wholeheartedly agreed. Holding the cloth, he felt a surge of determination. "We're going to get to the bottom of this, for Phineas, for Jim, for the ranch."

"The ranch!" Matthew suddenly felt a wave of sickness come over him. "Jed, I keep forgetting about the ranch. What are you going to do? You've got less than a week to figure something out."

"Matthew, I can't think about the ranch right now," Jedidiah said, his brow furrowed with concern. "Let's go inside and talk to Mr. Clayton. Maybe he saw something that can help us."

Inside the Davenport Dispatch & Delivery freight Company, they found Mr. Clayton, a middle-aged man with a stern expression, organizing paperwork behind the counter. He looked up as they entered, his eyes reflecting a mix of curiosity and apprehension.

"Mr. Clayton, we need to ask you about your encounter with Phineas Hargroves earlier," Jedidiah began, his voice firm. "Did you notice anything unusual or anyone suspicious when he arrived?"

Clayton leaned back, his gaze shifting as he recalled the morning's events. "Well, Jed, I saw this Hargroves fellow park his buggy out back but there was nothing out of the ordinary about that. I did however think it strange when I saw your foreman duck into the alley."

"Yes I know," Jedidiah replied, slightly irritated. "You made sure to tell the Sheriff how odd you thought it was."

"Well, after all, he did shoot him," Mr. Clayton suddenly became defensive. "Didn't he?"

"I'm not so sure that he did," Jedidiah suddenly realized that he might be coming off a bit defensive, considering his longtime friendship with Jim Davis. "We're just trying to figure out one way or another what happened."

"Well, I don't know what to tell you," the older man began gathering his paperwork up. "This Hargroves fellow came inside and told me he was looking for you. He followed me into my private office, despite my protests. I guess he thought I was hiding you in there."

"Did he tell you why he was so desperate to find me?"

"He started rambling about some miniature steam engine he said you created, but I couldn't make heads or tails about it!" Clayton replied.

"After that, he left and said he was going to keep looking for you."

"Did you see anyone follow him into the alley after he left?" Matthew interjected, eager for any clue.

Clayton paused, thinking hard. "The only person out of place this morning, besides Hargroves, was like I've already said, Jim Davis."

"Can you remember anything else? It could be crucial," Jedidiah urged.

"I'm afraid that's all I know, "Clayton replied, furrowing his brow.

"Thank you, Mr. Clayton," Jedidiah said, with very little hope in his voice.

As they left the office, Matthew and Jedidiah exchanged a determined look. "This doesn't seem promising," Jedidiah said, "But we're not giving up."

"Maybe we could talk to some of the men loading and unloading the wagons!" Matthew suggested a glimmer of hope in his eyes.

Jedidiah and Matthew approached the workers at the Davenport Dispatch & Delivery office, their presence drawing immediate attention. The workers, initially absorbed in their tasks, gradually slowed their movements, their expressions shifting from concentration to curiosity. A few exchanged wary glances, while others paused completely, tools in hand, clearly intrigued by the unexpected visit from the two men.

"Have any of you seen anything unusual today?" Jedidiah asked, studying their expressions for any sign of recognition.

One worker, a young man with a sunburnt face, stepped forward. He hesitated for a moment, nervously wiping his hands on his work apron. His voice was low and somewhat uncertain as he spoke, his eyes darting between Jedidiah and Matthew, betraying his unease. "Well, I might have seen something," he began cautiously, clearly unsure about speaking up.

Sensing his nervousness, Jedidiah stepped forward and tried to assure the man he would be doing the right thing by talking. "This is very important," he said. "A man's guilt or innocence could hang in the balance depending on what you saw."

The young man fidgeted around some more as if he was working up the nerve to say something. Finally, he said, "Well, maybe if you were to lay something in my palm," the young man extended his hand, "I might be more willing to speak."

"Well, if that's what it takes," Jedidiah replied with a steely gaze. "I'll be glad to lay some termination papers in your hand."

The young man suddenly decided to start talking, "I saw Mr. Davis and Mr. Hargroves before the shooting, but it didn't mean much to me then.

They didn't speak to each other. Mr. Hargroves followed Mr. Clayton inside, and Mr. Davis just turned and went towards the alley."

Matthew chimed in, "Did you notice anyone else around, maybe a third person who didn't belong?"

The workers exchanged glances, but no one else spoke. It was then that Jedidiah noticed the absence of a familiar face. "Where's Tom Miller?" he asked, remembering the young man he had met a few weeks ago.

"He left early today," another worker replied. "Said he wasn't feeling well."

Jedidiah and Matthew exchanged a knowing glance. Tom's disappearance, especially on such a chaotic day, seemed unusual. "Did he say what was wrong with him?"

"Didn't say a word!" the worker explained how they found out from Mr. Clayton that Tom had left early.

"Okay, well, thanks everyone," Jedidiah said, "If you think of anything else, let us know."

As they walked away, Matthew mused, "We should investigate this Tom Miller guy. His disappearance could be a coincidence, but it's worth looking into."

Jedidiah nodded in agreement. "Let's get his address from the company records and pay him a visit. It might be nothing, but right now, every piece of information could be vital."

The two men turned and went back inside the Davenport Dispatch & Delivery Company. They soon discovered that Mr. Clayton had gone out for the day and might not be coming back.

"We don't have time to wait around and find out if he's coming back!" Jedidiah announced as he led the way to Clayton's private office. "This is where all the company records are stored. If he provided us with an address, it'll be on file in here."

Jedidiah used his master key to unlock the door. He and Matthew, their resolve unwavering, entered. Clayton's desk, cluttered with paperwork and ledgers, seemed to conceal more than it revealed.

Jedidiah pointed towards the filing cabinet and said, "That's where they'll be!"

"I know, Jed," Matthew couldn't help but laugh. "You seem to forget that I'm the manager of your Sheffield branch and my office is set up the same way!"

"Oh yeah," Davenport began to laugh. "You've been away from there so long I guess I forgot."

"I hope that doesn't mean that I'm not going to have a job after we get everything straightened out."

"If we get everything straightened out," Jedidiah reluctantly corrected his friend. His confidence was finally beginning to waver. "But if we do, I promise you'll have a job for life with the

Davenport Dispatch & Delivery Company."

With that being said, they began their search with a sense of urgency, rifling through the employee records, and searching for any information on Tom Miller. The file cabinet creaked as they opened each drawer, the sound echoing in the quiet room.

As they sifted through the files, Matthew's hands moved with practiced efficiency, while Jedidiah's were slower and more deliberate, his brow furrowed in concentration. When they found Miller's file, Jedidiah's heart sank. Tom had not provided them with an address when he started working. Frustration etched on their faces, they stood in silence, the weight of their failure hanging heavy in the air.

As they prepared to leave, a faint, muffled noise stopped them in their tracks. It was coming from a large, old trunk in the corner of the room. They exchanged a look of confusion and alarm, the air thick with the musty scent of aged paper and wood.

"I think someone is in there!" Jedidiah exclaimed, his voice laced with urgency as he rushed over to examine it. He tried opening the lid but found it stubbornly locked, the metal was cold and unyielding under his fingers. Jedidiah stepped back, his heart pounding in his chest, as the sounds from inside the trunk grew more desperate.

Matthew, without a word, drew his revolver.

The air in the room seemed to freeze, punctuated only by the faint ticking of a clock on the wall. He aimed carefully and fired, the gunshot echoing deafeningly in the enclosed space, leaving a ringing silence in its wake.

They approached the trunk cautiously, the smell of gunpowder lingering in the air. As Jedidiah lifted the heavy lid, a figure bound and gagged emerged from the darkness, gasping for breath. It was Tom Miller, his eyes wide with a mix of fear and relief. He tried to stand, his movements hindered by his bonds, his clothing stained and disheveled.

As he rose, his strength faltered, and he collapsed, fainting into the arms of Jedidiah and Matthew!

CHAPTER XVII

The Witness

As Tom Miller collapsed into their arms, Jedidiah and Matthew lifted him out of the trunk and gently laid him on the floor.

"Matt help me get these off him," Jedidiah said, gesturing to the ropes binding Tom's wrists and ankles. Working quickly, they freed Tom from his constraints. His breaths were coming in short, ragged gasps as they removed the gag from his mouth.

"Get some water," Jedidiah barked, his voice a blend of concern and urgency.

As Matthew dashed to do as he was told, Jedidiah examined Tom more closely. His clothes were disheveled, and dark bruises were forming on his wrists where the ropes had dug in. Jedidiah's mind raced – how had Tom ended up bound and gagged in a trunk in Clayton's office?

Tom's eyes fluttered open and met Jedidiah's

with a mix of fear and confusion. "Mr. Davenport... they..." he croaked, his voice barely above a whisper.

"Easy now, Tom. Take it slow," Jedidiah said reassuringly, his hand resting on Tom's shoulder.

When Matthew returned, he handed the cup of water to Tom, who took it with trembling hands. After a few sips, his voice steadied slightly. "It was Mr. Clayton," he rasped. "He's the one who shot that man in the alley."

A chill ran down Jedidiah's spine at the thought of Mr. Clayton, a respected member of the community, committing such a crime. It was almost too much to believe. "Why would he shoot Phineas?"

"I have no idea," Tom replied, each word a struggle. "Mr. Clayton claimed it was because the old man was going to the bank to try and save your ranch, but that doesn't make sense."

Jedidiah exchanged a knowing glance with Matthew. The two men were completely stunned as the pieces of the puzzle came together to form a disturbing picture.

"Has Mr. Clayton been working with Elijah Perkins this whole time?" Matthew gasped.

"I don't know about anyone named Perkins," Tom replied, "but as he was tying me up, Mr. Clayton said he had to rush home and meet a fellow named Johnson."

"We need to let the sheriff know about this," Matthew said, with a firm voice.

"Agreed," Jedidiah replied. "Tom, can you walk?"

With their help, Tom slowly stood up, still shaky but determined. The three men made their way to Sheriff Thompson's office, the urgency of their mission lending strength to their steps.

Sheriff Thompson looked up, surprise evident on his face at their sudden entrance. "Jedidiah? What's going on? And what's happened to this young man?"

Jedidiah quickly relayed Tom's account, the Sheriff's expression growing graver with each word. "I'll issue a warrant for Clayton's arrest immediately," he declared, standing up. "This kind of treachery won't stand in our town."

Rushing over to the holding cell, Sheriff Thompson quickly unlocked the door and let Jim Davis out. Despite being under great stress, the ranch foreman had managed to fall asleep and hadn't heard any of the conversation that just took place.

"What's going on?" The framed man asked, groggily.

"I guess I owe you an apology," Sheriff Thompson said as he extended a hand to Jim, who took it, his face a mixture of relief and confusion.

"Apology accepted, Sheriff," he replied,

confused. "But what are you apologizing for?"

"For doubting your word about the shooting in the alley," Sheriff Thompson replied with a nod, "we now know for sure that you're innocent."

Jedidiah stepped forward, his voice steady but brimming with emotion. "It was Clayton," Jedidiah said, pausing as he saw the shock in Jim's eyes. "He's the one who shot Phineas!"

Jim's jaw clenched, his eyes narrowing as the sting of betrayal washed over him, hardening his expression. "Clayton? I can't believe it..." His voice trailed off, a look of anger and disbelief written all over his face.

"We've got no time to lose," Sheriff Thompson interjected, grabbing his hat and gun belt. "We need to bring Clayton in before he realizes we're onto him." He handed Jim Davis back his firearm and told him to come along.

The group hurried out of the sheriff's office, propelled forward by the urgency of the situation. The streets of the town were eerily quiet, effectively masking the storm that was about to unfold.

Approaching Clayton's house, Sheriff Thompson signaled for silence. They proceeded cautiously, each man highly aware of the potential danger that awaited them.

Jedidiah's thoughts were a whirlwind. Clayton's betrayal not only endangered him and his ranch but also struck the heart of the community. He felt a burning resolve to see justice done.

Sheriff Thompson knocked firmly on the door. "Clayton, open up, it's the Sheriff!"

"There's nobody inside!" Jedidiah shouted as he peeked through the window."

"Maybe he's gone back to the freight office!" Matthew suggested excitedly.

"Let's not waste time then," Sheriff Thompson said, turning swiftly toward the direction of the freight office. The group, now fueled by adrenaline and determination, followed him, moving quickly through the quiet streets.

Dusk was just beginning to set as the group neared the freight office. They knew they had to hurry as they would have very little daylight left. Upon rushing inside, they found that none of the workers had seen Mr. Clayton since he left earlier.

"As long as we're here," Sheriff Thompson turned to Tom Miller, "how about showing me exactly what you saw?"

Tom led them around back to an area just out of sight of the men loading the wagons. "This is where Mr. Clayton was crouching as he watched that Hargroves fellow walk up to Mr. Davis and speak to him. Mr. Clayton had a small pillow he brought with him from his office. He tried to muffle his shots with it, but it didn't help much."

"That would explain that piece of cloth we

found on the ground with the gunpowder burns!" Matthew Colton exclaimed.

"When Mr. Davis started shooting back, I couldn't help but gasp," Tom admitted reluctantly. "That's when Mr. Clayton turned around and saw me standing there. He stuck his gun in my side and forced me to sneak back inside."

"This certainly lines up with everything you said earlier, Jim," Sheriff Thompson said, glancing up at the tall, lanky man.

The ranch foreman merely smiled and nodded his head. "I knew I was innocent and you would eventually figure it out."

Matthew Colton suddenly spoke up, saying, "Now if we can just figure out where Clayton and Johnson went after they left Clayton's house."

"I wonder," Jedidiah suddenly began to muse, "was Clayton actually meeting him at his house, or was he just stopping by there on the way to meet him."

"That could have been what he meant," Tom Miller replied. "I'll admit I was a little preoccupied at the time, being bound and gagged, so I'm not one hundred percent sure."

"If that's the case, I think I know where he went..." Jedidiah looked off in deep thought for a moment.

Jim Davis reluctantly spoke up and said, "I think I do too."

The ranch owner and the ranch foreman turned to look at each other, eyes widening in mutual realization. In unison, they exclaimed, "Spoon Fork mine!"

"Spoon Fork mine," Sheriff Thompson echoed his brow furrowing in thought. "It's been abandoned for years. Why would they go there?"

Jedidiah's gaze was firm. "It's isolated, and they probably thought it would be the last place we'd look. It's the perfect hideout."

"You seem pretty confident," Sheriff Thompson stated, staring directly into Jedidiah's eyes. "What makes you so sure?"

"That's because Matt, Phineas, and I found them there yesterday," Jedidiah shrugged.

"Well, that's a pretty good clue," Sheriff Thompson chuckled.

"And that's where we're headed now," declared Matthew, his determination mirrored in the faces of the others.

The group quickly organized themselves, gathering necessary supplies for the trek to the Spoon Fork mine. The air was filled with a sense of urgency, each member understanding the stakes of their mission.

Sheriff Thompson insisted that Tom Miller stay behind. "Go over to Doc's office and get yourself checked out!" he ordered the boy.

With the addition of Sheriff Thompson's

deputies, the remaining members of the group left town and ventured into the night. The rugged landscape stretched out before them.

The journey to the mine was treacherous, the path overgrown and barely visible. But Jedidiah and Jim, familiar with the land, led the way confidently, their knowledge of the terrain proving invaluable.

The Spoon Fork mine loomed ahead, its entrance a dark maw, the cool air emanating from it mingling with the earthy scent of damp soil. With cautious steps, the group advanced, each aware of the looming presence of Clayton and Johnson inside.

Sheriff Thompson signaled for quiet as they neared the entrance. "We need to be careful," he whispered. "There's no telling what we're walking into."

Jedidiah nodded, raising his rifle. "Let's stick together. We'll cover more ground and watch each other's backs."

As they slipped into the mine, their cautious steps were muffled by the thick dust on the ground. The musty scent of damp earth and the coolness of the air intensified the eeriness of their silent advance, with the remnants of the mine's past life evident in the abandoned tools and carts that littered the path.

As they delved deeper, the tension grew. Every

shadow seemed to move, every noise made them pause. But they pressed on, determined to bring Clayton and Johnson to justice.

Suddenly, a noise up ahead caught their attention. They froze, listening intently. The sound of voices, muffled but unmistakable, reached their ears.

"This is it," Jedidiah whispered. "They're just up ahead."

With a collective nod, they moved forward, ready to confront whatever awaited them.

The dim light from the lanterns attached to the walls barely pierced the darkness of the mine. Each step forward was cautious, and calculated. The muffled voices grew louder, a heated conversation taking place just around the bend.

As they edged closer, Jedidiah signaled for the group to spread out, creating a wider perimeter. Sheriff Thompson and his deputies flanked to the left, while Jedidiah, Jim, and Matthew took the right. The tension was thick, a heavy blanket in the cool, underground air.

Peering around the corner, they could see Clayton and Johnson, deep in discussion by the flickering light of a single lantern. They were facing each other, unaware of the impending confrontation. None of Johnson's gang appeared to be with them.

Sheriff Thompson gestured for his men to hold

Clayton and Johnson were unaware
of the impending confrontation.

position, waiting for the right moment to strike. Jedidiah exchanged a nod with Jim and Matthew, the unspoken agreement clear between them.

Leroy's voice echoed through the mine, tinged with anger. "You really expect me to clean up your mess?" He shook his head in disbelief. "I had nothing to do with you shooting that crazy old man!"

"I just need you to ride into Spoon Fork and help me do away with the kid who saw me do it." Mr. Clayton's expression became more intent. "After all, didn't I help you by planting that explosive under the safe in the freight office?"

"That was for your benefit as well as mine!" Johnson retorted.

"What about you giving me that pocket watch to plant in the debris?" Clayton was growing impatient. "That was strictly your idea. You thought if you framed your old friend you could force him to join up with you!"

Upon hearing this, Jedidiah quickly turned to look at his foreman. The latter merely nodded in acknowledgment. Jim Davis had suspected that Leroy was the one who had stolen his watch. He remembered that Leroy had come to the ranch a few days before the explosion, attempting to persuade him to join his gang.

"Well, that plan failed miserably," Johnson retorted. "He came to see me in town numerous times but never came down off his high horse. Jim actually tried to get me to cut ties with Perkins and lay off Davenport."

"Oh yes," Clayton began, nodding his head. "Speaking of Elijah Perkins, I figure he owes me one!"

"How do you figure that?"

"Who do you think tipped him off about Jedidiah taking out the loan on his ranch?"

Jedidiah's jaw nearly dropped as it suddenly dawned on him. The memory of Clayton lurking near the bank president's door on the day he took out the loan flashed before him. "He was there all along," Jedidiah realized, as an additional sense of betrayal washed over him.

Johnson pushed his hat back on his head and started laughing. "So that was you? Seems like you're more crooked and underhanded than I ever was!"

"Just the same, Perkins owes me one!"

"Do I look like Perkins?" Leroy Johnson was not one to be intimidated. "That's between you and him!"

Deciding he had heard enough, Sheriff Thompson gave everyone the signal. With a sudden rush, they moved in. "Clayton! Johnson! You're surrounded!" Sheriff Thompson's voice boomed through the cavern, echoing off the walls.

Startled, Clayton and Johnson spun around,

their faces registering shock and fear. Clayton reached for his weapon, but Jedidiah already had his rifle trained on the man.

"There's nowhere to run, Clayton," Jedidiah said, his voice steady and commanding. "You're going to answer for what you've done."

Johnson, seeing the hopelessness of their situation, dropped his weapon and raised his hands in surrender. Clayton, however, hesitated, his eyes darting around, looking for an escape route that didn't exist.

Sheriff Thompson stepped forward, his deputies following suit. "You're under arrest for the attempted murder of Phineas Hargroves, the explosion at the freight office, and the conspiracy to frame Jim Davis."

Clayton's shoulders slumped in defeat, and he finally relinquished his weapon, allowing the deputies to handcuff him. Johnson followed suit, a look of resignation on his face.

As they led the two men out of the mine, Jedidiah couldn't help but feel a sense of relief mixed with exhaustion. The truth had finally come to light, and justice was within reach.

The ride back to town was quiet, the group's thoughts as heavy as the night around them. Jedidiah rode at the front, his mind racing over the night's events, while the rest followed without a word. The only sound breaking the oppressive silence was the steady rhythm of the horses' hoofbeats.

By the time they arrived back on the familiar dusty streets of Spoon Fork, it was nearly ten o'clock. The dim outlines of buildings began to emerge as they neared the town, and lanterns flickered in the darkness, casting a soft glow on the deserted streets. The town seemed to be sleeping, unaware of the storm that had just passed.

Sheriff Thompson broke the silence as they approached his office. "Well, that's one part of this mess sorted," he said, a hint of weariness in his voice. "Now let's see what comes next."

Dismounting in front of the building, the familiar surroundings provided a stark contrast to the tension of the mine. The door to the sheriff's office creaked open, sounding loud in the quiet of the night.

Inside, the office felt like a safe haven after the chaos at Spoon Fork mine. It was a return to something resembling normalcy, but Jedidiah knew there was still more to be done.

Sheriff Thompson and his two deputies promptly locked both Clayton and Johnson into a cell. He thanked his deputies for their help and told them they could go home and get some rest.

"I guess you'll be going after Elijah Perkins tomorrow," Jedidiah assumed. He, Matthew Colton, and Jim Davis gathered around Sheriff Thompson's desk and waited for his reply.

"On what grounds?" the Sheriff asked, leaning back in his chair. "All those two admitted to was working to help Perkins buy your ranch. Their methods were crooked and underhanded, but nothing they said tied him directly to any criminal activity."

"So once again, there's nothing I can do but sit and wait for him to foreclose and take everything from me!"

"Jed, my hands are tied." Sheriff Thompson's face showed genuine regret. "I have to do everything by..."

"The law, I know!" Jedidiah finished his sentence.

"Jed, I know it still seems hopeless," Sheriff Thompson said, trying to find the right words to comfort his friend. "But there's still time. Don't give up now."

Just as the young entrepreneur was about to respond, the door to the Sheriff's office swung open, and Tom Miller came storming inside. "Come quick!" he shouted.

"Now hold on, young fellow!" Sheriff Thompson stood to his feet. "What's this all about? Where are we going?"

Tom had run from the doctor's office after spotting the group of men riding into town. "Doc Stone sent me to fetch you. It's Mr. Hargroves!"

CHAPTER XVIII

The Final Revelation

The door to the doctor's office swung open with a sense of urgency as Jedidiah, Sheriff Thompson, and the others burst in, their boots echoing on the wooden floor. The smell of antiseptics filled the air, mixing with the faint aroma of herbal remedies. The office was dimly lit, its walls lined with shelves of medical supplies and books.

"How is he, Doc?" Jedidiah asked, his voice heavy with concern as they gathered around Phineas Hargroves' bed.

Doc Stone, a man of few words but great skill, turned from his patient, wiping his hands on a cloth. "He's awake and conscious," he announced with a hint of relief in his usually stoic expression. "Gave us quite a scare, but he's going to be okay. Just needs more rest."

A collective sigh of relief escaped the group. Jim Davis stepped closer, his eyes studying

Phineas' face, searching for signs of the ordeal he had been through.

Hargroves, though pale and visibly tired, managed a weak smile. "Seems I've caused a bit of a commotion," he murmured, his voice barely above a whisper.

"You sure did, Phineas," Matthew Colton replied, a warm smile on his face. "You've got a strong heart in you."

Jedidiah leaned in, his eyes reflecting a mix of relief and gratitude. "You had us worried there, but we're glad you're pulling through."

Phineas tried to nod, but his movements sluggish. "Had to... survive," he breathed out. "Couldn't let... Perkins and his cronies... win."

Sheriff Thompson, who had been standing quietly by the door, stepped forward. "Your determination is something else, Mr. Hargroves. It's a relief to see you're on the mend."

Doc Stone cleared his throat, drawing their attention. "He needs to rest now. No more excitement for today. You all should head home and get some rest too."

The group nodded in understanding, each taking a moment to pat Phineas' hand or offer a word of encouragement before slowly filing out of the room.

Before they walked out the door, Phineas looked directly at Jim Davis and thanked him for trying to save his life in the alley. Jim merely smiled and nodded his head.

As they stepped back into the cool night air, the reality of what had transpired over the past few hours seemed to sink in. They had faced darkness, uncovered truths, and now, witnessed a friend's resilience in the face of adversity.

Jedidiah took a deep breath, the night's events weighing heavily on him. "Tomorrow's another day," he said, more to himself than to the others. "We'll see what it brings."

****

The next morning, light streamed through the kitchen window, casting a warm glow over the breakfast table where Jedidiah Davenport and Matthew Colton sat. The clatter of cutlery and the aroma of freshly brewed coffee filled the room. Despite the comfort of the morning routine, there was a sense of urgency in the air.

Jedidiah, looking more rested but still burdened by the previous day's events, sipped his coffee thoughtfully. "I can't imagine today will be any easier," he said, breaking the silence. His eyes briefly met Matthew's, a mutual understanding of the challenges ahead reflected in their gaze.

Matthew, while buttering his toast, nodded in agreement. "We've stirred up quite the hornet's nest,

Jed. Clayton and Johnson being locked up is only the start. Perkins is still out there, and he won't take kindly to his plans unraveling."

Jedidiah leaned back in his chair, his mind racing through the possible scenarios they might face in town. "We need to keep our eyes open," he mused. "Perkins won't go down without a fight, and he's got enough influence to make things difficult for us."

Matthew took a thoughtful bite of his toast. "Do you think Phineas will remember more about what happened? Maybe something that can tie Perkins directly to all this?"

"That's the hope," Jedidiah replied, finishing his coffee. "Once Phineas is up to it, we need to have a proper talk with him. But for now, our priority is to keep the town safe and stand our ground."

Finishing their breakfast, they rose from the table, their movements efficient and purposeful. Jedidiah grabbed his hat from the rack, his expression determined. "Let's head into town. We've got a long day ahead."

Matthew picked up his hat and followed. "After yesterday, Spoon Fork won't be the same again!"

Stepping out into the brisk morning air, Jedidiah and Matthew mounted their horses. After about an hour's ride, the town's silhouette started becoming visible in the distance against the lightning sky. The ride into Spoon Fork had been quiet, each man lost in his thoughts, mentally preparing for the day's challenges.

As they arrived in town, the streets were just coming to life, the townspeople starting their day, unaware of the undercurrents shifting beneath the surface. Jedidiah and Matthew exchanged a determined look, ready to face whatever the day would bring.

Jedidiah steered his horse towards the Doctor's office, his mind preoccupied with the tasks ahead; the unavoidable confrontation with Perkins was in the back of his mind.

Matthew, riding alongside, broke the silence. "Jed, you think the town knows about Clayton and Johnson, yet?"

"I'm sure some do, word travels fast," Jedidiah replied. "But to the full extent of what took place, who knows?"

As they dismounted in front of the Doctor's office, Doc Stone greeted them, his face etched with the strain of dealing with a difficult stubborn patient. "Morning, Jed, Matthew. If you're looking for Hargroves, he's not here."

"Not here?" Jedidiah Davenport was taken aback by these words. "Where is he?"

"He said he had business to take care of over at the bank!" The doctor replied, "I warned him it was too soon for him to be up gallivanting around like that, but he wouldn't listen to me!"

"Do you suppose he's going to do whatever he had planned yesterday?" Matthew asked curiously.

Jedidiah's thoughts raced as he suddenly remembered the remark that Tom Miller had made about Phineas being on the way to the bank to save his ranch. "What could he possibly be up to?"

Not even bothering to remount their horses, Jedidiah Davenport and Matthew Colton dashed down the street on foot to the Spoon Fork bank. Once inside, they spotted Mr. Simmons and Phineas B. Hargroves in a heated discussion with none other than Elijah Perkins.

The tension in the air was thick as Jedidiah and Matthew Colton burst through the bank's doors, their arrival drawing the attention of everyone present.

Phineas Hargroves, standing firm despite his evident frailty, held a piece of paper in his hand – the bank draft that Jedidiah had made out to him in payment for the blueprints and patent for his airship design. His voice, though weak, carried a determined edge. "Mr. Simmons, as I was trying to explain, this draft is for the exact amount of Jedidiah's loan."

Elijah Perkins, standing opposite Phineas, was visibly agitated, his usual composure crumbling under the weight of the unfolding events. "This is preposterous! That draft was issued under different circumstances. It's not valid for this purpose!"

Mr. Simmons, the bank manager, adjusted his glasses, examining the draft carefully. His expression was one of cautious scrutiny. After a moment, he looked up, his voice steady. "Mr. Perkins, I've reviewed this document and the original loan agreement. Legally, I'm obligated to accept this as payment. The loan against Mr. Davenport's ranch will be marked paid in full."

"What about interest?" Perkins' eyes suddenly lit up, thinking for a moment that he had the old man.

"According to the agreement," Mr. Simmons smiled, "interest doesn't start accumulating until after the first ninety days. It hasn't even been thirty days, yet. Therefore, you have zero interest due on the loan."

Perkins' face reddened with anger, but he was powerless in the face of the bank's decision. Jedidiah stepped forward, his gaze fixed on Perkins. "It looks like things didn't quite work out as you planned."

Matthew, standing beside Jedidiah, couldn't help but feel a sense of triumph. The tables had turned, and justice was finally being served.

Phineas, with a supportive nod from Jedidiah, handed the draft to Mr. Simmons. "Let it be known that this act is not just about saving a ranch. It's about preserving the integrity of an entire valley against men like Perkins."

The bank manager nodded, beaming with pride as he accepted the draft. "I'll process this immediately. Mr. Davenport, your ranch is safe."

The room fell into a hushed silence as the reality of the moment sank in. Perkins, defeated, turned and walked out of the bank, his plans in ruins. The townspeople, who had gathered to witness the exchange, broke into murmurs, the tide of public opinion turning against Perkins.

Just before Elijah Perkins stepped out, he turned back and proclaimed, "This is far from over. I will have that property in my hands one way or another!"

After he watched the railroad tyrant exit the building, Jedidiah turned to Phineas, extending his hand in gratitude. "Phineas, I can't thank you enough. You've saved more than just my ranch today."

Phineas, leaning heavily on a cane, managed a tired but satisfied smile. "It was the right thing to do, Jed. This town needs more than just one person to look out for it."

"But what about your money?" Jedidiah asked, hesitantly. "That was all the payment you asked for your plans, the patent, and overseeing the project."

"My dear boy, it was the least I could do," Hargroves replied. "After all, it's partly my fault you were in this mess." His face suddenly broke into a wide smile. "Besides, seeing the expression

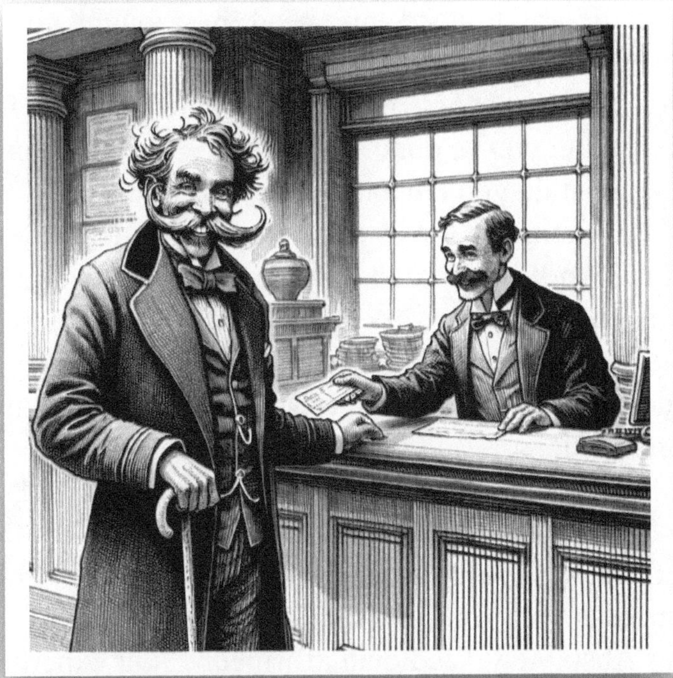

The bank manager nodded, beaming
with pride as he accepted the draft.

on that man's face was all the payment I needed."

Jedidiah dropped his head in thought for a moment and made Phineas B. Hargroves a proposal. "What if I offered you something else for everything you've done?"

"What do you have in mind, dear boy?"

"In exchange for your blueprints, the patent, and all the work you've done over the past few weeks, I want to offer you 25% of the profits from all new business brought in through the airships. Additionally, I'd like you to stay on, overseeing the construction of each one, with a regular salary."

The room fell silent, all eyes on Phineas. His eyes widened slightly, clearly taken aback by the generous offer. "Jedidiah, that's more than generous. Are you sure?"

"Absolutely," Jedidiah affirmed, "Your expertise is invaluable, and you deserve a share in what we're building. Together, we can take this venture to new heights."

Phineas nodded, a slow smile forming on his lips. "Then you have a deal, Jedidiah."

Jedidiah and Phineas exchanged a look of mutual respect and understanding, knowing they had just begun a powerful partnership. Matthew clapped Jedidiah on the back, "Looks like things are starting to look up!"

Jedidiah nodded, his gaze following Perkins' retreating figure down the streets of Spoon Fork.

"Yeah, they are, Matt, but I have a feeling it's still not over."

Elijah Perkins, lost in anger and oblivious to his surroundings, walked straight into Sheriff Thompson, who had just stepped into the street from his office.

"Watch where you're going!" Elijah snapped at the lawman.

Thompson, never one to back down, replied, "Watch where I'm going? Seems to me that you were the one not paying attention to where you were going!"

Perkins whirled around to face him but realized for the first time that he had been talking to the law. He suddenly took on a more submissive tone. "You're absolutely right, Marshal. I should be watching where I'm going."

"Sheriff!" Thompson stated firmly. "I don't recall seeing you around town. What's your name?"

"Perkins, Elijah Perkins," the executive for the D.&R.W. Railroad suddenly seemed nervous.

"I guess you're here to bail your men out of jail."

"My men?" Perkins' confidence suddenly returned. "I don't know what you're talking about."

"Clayton and Johnson." Sheriff Thompson pointed towards his office. "Got them both locked up in there."

"Marshal... I mean Sheriff, those men are in no

way connected to me or the railroad."

"Not according to them. The way they tell it..."

"Sheriff!" Perkins interrupted the lawman angrily, "I don't care what they say. They're no employees of mine. Therefore, they can rot in jail, for all I care!" As he said this, he turned and headed down the street where his buggy and driver were waiting for him. Within moments, he was riding out of town.

Jedidiah, who had watched the whole thing, turned to Matthew and asked him to hitch up the buggy that was still at the freight office. That way Phineas could go back to the ranch and rest. "Jim can ride with him, but for now I want him to come with me."

As he watched Matthew and Phineas walking away, Jedidiah turned to Jim Davis and motioned for him to follow him into the Sheriff's office. They walked in just in time to see Sheriff Thompson relaying the message from Perkins about them rotting in jail.

"If there is anything the two of you can tell us that can incriminate him," Sheriff Thompson said, "you need to speak up now."

"I can't believe Perkins would abandon us like this!" Johnson scoffed in disbelief.

"Leroy, I just saw Elijah Perkins ride out of town." Jim Davis tried one more time to talk some reason into his old friend. "He has no intention of rescuing either of you. Now for once in your life do the right thing and tell us something we can use to stop him!"

"If you do," Sheriff Thompson spoke up, "I guarantee the Judge will go easier on you."

Leroy Johnson thought about these words for a moment, then said, "I don't know what, but there's something valuable about that land of yours, Davenport. Perkins never wanted it for the railroad. He wanted it for himself, but he never would tell any of us why."

"That would explain why the bill of sale he's been trying to force me to sign was made out directly to him and not the railroad," Jedidiah remarked, his suspicions becoming confirmed. "The only bill of sale I've seen made out to the D.&R.W. Railroad was the one I've said this whole time was a much more obvious choice for the track."

"That's right!" Johnson quickly added. "And all the deeds to the land he put barricades on to block your wagons were made out to him too."

"This is all starting to make sense," Sheriff Thompson stepped back, reflecting in thought.

"You don't know what it is about my land that he finds so valuable?" Jedidiah asked, curiously.

"All I know is that it's somehow connected to the Spoon Fork mine," Johnson continued, divulging everything. "Perkins initially hired me and my boys to reopen the mine after he purchased it. It didn't take us long to realize it was pointless, but Perkins wouldn't take our word for it. He decided to check it out for himself. One day, he went into the shaft and disappeared. We didn't see him again until late the next day. When he came back, it was with a whole new purpose, and that was to own your land!"

CHAPTER XIX

The Escape

"It's somehow connected to the Spoon Fork Mine," Johnson's words resonated in Jedidiah's mind, igniting a spark of realization.

Jim Davis, noticing the change in Jedidiah's expression, leaned in. "Jed, what is it? You look like you've seen a ghost."

"I've got it!" Jedidiah's voice rose with excitement. "The exit tunnel comes out in the middle of my property. The very same parcel that Perkins has been after this whole time. What if he's not after the land itself but what's beneath it?"

Sheriff Thompson, with a look of doubt on his face, asked, "You think there's gold under your property?"

"I'm not saying there is," Jedidiah replied, "but it would make sense if there were. Either way, he must have found something valuable on my land. Why else would he have gone to all this trouble?"

Jim Davis nodded in agreement, his mind working through the possibilities. "I've seen gold fever make men do some crazy things."

Jedidiah turned to Leroy Johnson and asked, "When Perkins came out of the mine, did he say anything that might give us a clue?"

Johnson shrugged, a look of confusion on his face. "Not much. Just kept muttering about 'a new beginning' and 'untapped potential.' He was different, obsessed."

"Our next move is clear," Jedidiah declared, his resolve firming. "When Matthew returns, we're heading straight back to the Spoon Fork Mine."

"How come?" Sheriff Thompson asked confused, "You already know it comes out on the parcel of land that Perkins has been trying to take from you."

"That's true," Davenport admitted, "but not the exact spot and that's where I need to look."

Without any further discussion, Jim Davis was sent out to take Matthew's place in bringing Phineas Hargroves back to the ranch. As soon as Colton returned, the two men started riding toward their old childhood playground.

As they approached the mine, they once again recalled the day they found the exit tunnel. A day of fear and adventure that had bonded them as brothers. Neither could have imagined that the same tunnel would be key to their current predicament.

Reaching the entrance, they dismounted and equipped themselves with lanterns. They exchanged a determined look and stepped inside. The cool, damp air enveloped them. They made their way through familiar passages, their footsteps echoing in the silence.

Hours later, they reached the area where the hidden exit tunnel lay—just as they remembered, a narrow passage barely visible against the walls of the mine.

"This is it," Matthew said in a low voice. "This is where we found our way out."

Jedidiah nodded, his lantern casting shadows on the walls. "Maybe now we'll find out why Perkins has been so obsessed with my land."

They stepped out into the sunlight, the beauty of the valley stark against the darkness they had left behind.

Jedidiah looked around, seeing his land with new eyes. "If Perkins found this tunnel, he's had a direct, hidden route to the heart of my property, this whole time."

Matthew looked at the surrounding landscape, his mind working through the implications. "We need to figure out what he discovered that's so valuable about this place."

Jedidiah and Matthew spent the next several hours scouring the area around the exit of the tunnel, looking for any signs that could explain Perkins' interest in the land. They searched for indications of gold or any other valuable minerals by inspecting rocks, soil, and the walls of the tunnel exit.

Despite their meticulous efforts, they found nothing out of the ordinary. The land appeared just as it always had – rugged, and beautiful, but seemingly unremarkable in terms of mineral wealth.

As the sun began its descent, casting long shadows over the valley, a sense of disappointment settled over them. Matthew sighed, wiping the sweat from his brow. "I don't get it, Jed. There's nothing here. No sign of gold, nothing that would drive a man like Perkins to such lengths."

Jedidiah, equally frustrated, kicked at a small rock. "I was so sure we were onto something. But it looks like we're back to square one."

They were about to call it a day when Matthew decided to explore a dense area covered in brush, a few yards from the tunnel exit. "Let's just check this last spot before we head back," he called out to Jedidiah.

As Matthew stepped onto the brush-covered ground, the seemingly solid earth beneath him gave way unexpectedly. With a startled yell, he fell through the hidden opening, disappearing from Jedidiah's sight.

With a startled yell, he fell
through the hidden opening.

"Matthew!" Jedidiah rushed over, his heart pounding with sudden fear. Peering into the hole, he saw his friend sitting in a shallow pool of dark liquid.

"What's all this stuff?" Matthew asked, looking down at his soaked boots and pants. The liquid was thick and had a distinct, pungent odor.

Jedidiah quickly found a safe way to climb down and join his friend. As he reached the bottom, the smell became overwhelming. "This... this is oil!" Jedidiah exclaimed, realization dawning on him.

Matthew, still trying to make sense of his unexpected fall, looked around. He was sitting in what appeared to be a natural oil seep, hidden just beneath the surface of the dirt. "Oil... all this time, it was oil!"

"I knew it!" Jedidiah exclaimed, jumping up and down. "This is what he's been after this whole time!" He stopped celebrating, leaned over, and extended a hand to help Matthew stand up. "We've got to get back to town and let Sheriff Thompson know about this!" he declared.

The sun began to set as they made their way back to the tunnel exit. Treading carefully through the familiar underground passage, Jedidiah and Matthew felt a mix of exhaustion and anticipation. Hours later, they emerged at the other end. With nightfall now upon them, the discovery of the oil seep under Jedidiah's land weighed heavily on their minds as they stepped out into the wide-open space.

By the time Jedidiah and Matthew made it back to town, the streets of Spoon Fork were quiet and deserted, with only a few lanterns flickering in the darkness. They steered their horses toward the sheriff's office, each man lost in thought about the day's revelations.

Upon reaching the office, Jedidiah dismounted with a sense of urgency. He knocked on the door firmly, signaling their arrival. Sheriff Thompson, who had been working late, opened the door with a look of surprise. "Jedidiah, Matthew, what brings you here at this hour?"

"We've found something, Sheriff," Jedidiah said, his voice tense with the gravity of their discovery.

"Don't tell me you actually found gold on your property?" Sheriff Thompson was taken aback in surprise as he returned to his desk and sat down.

"No," Jedidiah laughed, shaking his head.

Thompson didn't show any sign of surprise at this reply. He simply nodded, his expression thoughtful. "I didn't think so," he said, his voice carrying a note of confirmation. "Folks have worked that mine for years and never found anything more substantial than the initial strike that drove them to form the mine in the first place."

"We didn't find gold, but we did find something," Jedidiah's eyes began to sparkle with enthusiasm. "We found something big."

Thompson leaned back in his chair, his eyes narrowing with interest. "What did you find?"

"We found oil!" Matthew shouted, his impetuous nature unable to contain itself any longer. "A natural oil seep right under the land Perkins has been after this whole time!"

Thompson's eyebrows shot up in surprise. "Oil? That's what this has been about?"

"Seems so," Jedidiah replied. "It explains everything - his obsession, the lengths he's gone to. Oil could bring a fortune, change the whole landscape here."

Thompson stood up, his mind already racing with the implications. "This is big, Jed. If Perkins does know about this, there's no telling what he might do next. We need to be prepared and start planning our next move."

"If Phineas is up to traveling tomorrow," Jedidiah spoke thoughtfully, "I want him to inspect the oil seep and see if it's really as valuable as I think it is."

"Whether it is or it isn't," Sheriff Thompson stated excitedly, "if we can prove that Perkins knew about it, we might just have a case against him!"

****

The next morning, with the first rays of dawn filtering through the windows, Jedidiah Davenport and Matthew Colton sat at the breakfast table with Phineas Hargroves. The old, eccentric inventor listened intently, his eyes widening in surprise as they recounted their discovery of the oil seep.

"My dear boy," Phineas murmured, his mind visibly working through the implications. "Oil, you say? Underneath your land? That's quite the turn of events."

"It sure is," Jedidiah replied, his voice laced with a mixture of excitement and concern. "We need your expertise, Phineas. We have to confirm what we've found and understand exactly what we're dealing with."

Phineas nodded, his expression turning serious. "I'll need to see it for myself, but if what you're saying is true, this could be a game-changer."

Matthew leaned forward, his hands gripping tightly to his coffee cup. "But we've got to move carefully. If Perkins gets wind that we're onto him, there's no telling what he might do."

Jedidiah sighed, his gaze steady. "That's why we need to be one step ahead. We need to confirm the oil seep is as valuable as we think it is. After that, we can figure out our next move. We just need to do it quickly and quietly."

"My dear boy," Phineas said, pushing back his

chair. "If this discovery of yours is anything like you say it is, I don't think you'll have to worry about Elijah Perkins ever again."

Jedidiah let out a resounding sigh of relief, suddenly rejuvenated with newfound hope.

The three men quickly finished their breakfast and started towards the area of the ranch where Jedidiah's and Phineas' two airships were kept.

Helping the older man into the buggy for the ride out there, Jedidiah asked, "Are you sure you're up to the trip?"

"After all you were wounded just two days ago," Matthew quickly added.

"My dear boys," Phineas replied boastfully. "It takes more than a single bullet to slow me down!"

Upon arriving at the airship hangar, Jedidiah announced that he would run inside and get the steam engine started to open the roof.

"Let's take my craft this time," Hargroves remarked as he climbed from the buggy. He pointed to his airship parked near the side of the building. "The Icarus hasn't had a chance to soar in nearly a month now. It's high time we let the old boy stretch his wings," he declared, with a twinkle in his eye.

Jedidiah and Matthew exchanged a knowing glance, both aware of Phineas' fondness for his creation. They helped the old inventor aboard the airship, a magnificent vessel that bore the marks of

Phineas' genius and eccentricity. The Icarus, with its intricate network of gears and polished brass fittings, stood ready, its presence as commanding as ever.

As Jedidiah fired up the engines, the airship came to life with a series of mechanical whirs and hisses, the propellers starting their rhythmic dance. Matthew took his place beside Jedidiah, while Phineas settled into a chair, his eyes bright with excitement.

The Icarus lifted gracefully into the sky, the landscape below gradually shrinking as they ascended. The morning light bathed the valley in a warm glow, the view from above revealing the sprawling beauty of Jedidiah's land.

Within what felt like practically no time at all, they were hovering over the site of the oil seep. Jedidiah expertly maneuvered the airship for a closer look. From their vantage point, the hidden secrets of the land below were laid bare. The exit of the mine tunnel, now a significant spot, was visible amidst the rugged terrain.

Phineas leaned over, his keen eyes examining the area. "Remarkable," he muttered, lowering his goggles over his eyes for a better view. "Let's get a closer look from the ground."

Jedidiah guided the Icarus to a gentle landing near the site. The trio disembarked, with Matthew leading the way. After he was helped down into the hidden cavern, Hargroves crouched down, his fingers tracing the ground as he inspected the dark liquid pooled in the shallow depression.

"This is indeed oil," confirmed Phineas, his voice a mix of awe and seriousness. "A natural reservoir, hidden away from prying eyes. Jedidiah, this discovery... it's more than just valuable. It's a power shift."

Jedidiah nodded, the reality of their find settling in.

Phineas stood up, his gaze meeting Jedidiah's. "If you don't mind me taking over, I have a plan. Our next move is to have a meeting with the board of directors of the D.&R.W. Railroad."

Jedidiah exchanged a knowing glance with Matthew. "The board of directors? What are you planning, Phineas?" he inquired, intrigued by the sudden shift in strategy.

Phineas, grinning slyly, adjusted his goggles atop his cap. "My dear boys, sometimes the best way to deal with a snake is to go straight into its den. We need to confront them and show them what we've found. If my hunch is correct, the board has no clue as to what Perkins has really been up to. Even if they do, it'll put him on the defensive, and we can use that to our advantage."

With a newfound sense of urgency, Jedidiah, Matthew, and Phineas re-boarded the airship and piloted the Icarus towards Hawthorn Grove, the location of the D.&R.W. Railroad headquarters. The airship, slicing through the sky with graceful determination, carried them swiftly to their destination.

Upon arrival, they landed the vessel in a nearby field. Without wasting a moment, they made a beeline for the headquarters, a formidable two-story building that stood as a testament to the railroad's influence.

As they entered, Jedidiah led the way, his face set in a mask of resolve. "Is Perkins in?" He demanded to know.

"Perkins is upstairs, with the entire board," a secretary replied, her eyes wide with surprise at their sudden appearance.

Without hesitation, all three of them stormed up the stairs and barged into the office, interrupting the meeting. The board members looked up in shock and Perkins' face turned a shade paler at their sight.

"What's the meaning of this?" Perkins shouted. He stood to his feet and started screaming for a guard.

"Just a minute!" Phineas B. Hargroves stepped forward. "We came here to say something, and we're going to say it!"

"Why should we listen to what you have to say?" one of the board members asked.

"Because it's something that affects every one of you," Jedidiah announced authoritatively. "We have proof that someone has been embezzling funds from this company!" As he said this, the room fell into a hushed silence, all eyes fixed on him.

"This is ridiculous!" Perkins shouted. "Let's get him out of here!"

"Just a minute, Elijah!" A man who would later be identified as the chairman of the board, said, "I want to hear what these people have to say!" Every member of the board sitting there agreed with him. Elijah Perkins had no choice but to stand back and let them speak.

For the next several minutes, Jedidiah, aided by interjections from Matthew and Phineas, laid everything out – the discovery of the oil seep, all the properties purchased under Perkins' name, and the one significant property bought under the railroad's name. "This one," Jedidiah pointed towards a section of land on the map laid out on the table in front of them, "hasn't even been recorded at the land office yet."

Matthew stepped forward, his oil-stained clothes tangible evidence of their discovery. "Perkins has been playing all of you. He's been using railroad money for his own personal gain."

The board members began to murmur among themselves, the gravity of the accusations sinking in. Perkins tried to interject, but the evidence was overwhelming.

"Why hasn't it been recorded yet?" one of the board members asked. "That's the property we all voted on from day one!"

Caught off guard, the railroad executive fumbled over his words.

One of the directors stood up, anger etched on his face. "This is an egregious misuse of company funds and a breach of trust. We cannot let this stand. Perkins, you are to be arrested for your actions."

Perkins' face twisted in panic. As the board members called for armed guards, he suddenly bolted towards the window. With a desperate leap, he flung himself off the balcony!

CHAPTER XX

A New Beginning

As Perkins leaped from the balcony, a collective gasp echoed through the room. The board members and the trio rushed to the window, only to see Perkins miraculously landing on a hay cart conveniently parked below, effectively cushioning his fall. In a matter of seconds, he rolled off the cart, rushed through the crowd of railroad workers, and disappeared into the woods surrounding the area.

"Quick, after him!" Jedidiah shouted, the adrenaline surging through his veins. Matthew and the armed guards were right on his heels as they raced down the stairs and out of the building.

They scoured the surrounding area for over twenty minutes before giving up the chase.

"Lost him," Matthew panted, coming to a stop beside Jedidiah. "He's vanished like a ghost."

Davenport, catching his breath, adjusted his cap

As Perkins leaped from the balcony, a collective gasp echoed through the room.

and said, "He may have slipped away for now, but he won't get far. We've exposed him, and after today he's going to be a wanted man."

Returning to the main building, they rejoined Phineas B. Hargroves in Perkins' office. He had been filling the board in on the events of his shooting, the roadblocks, and other nefarious events organized by men under the former railroad executive's employment.

The chairman of the board, an older man with a weathered face, stepped forward and spoke, "We've been deceived by Perkins, and for bringing this deception to light, we owe you a debt of gratitude. Rest assured, the D.&R.W. Railroad will fully cooperate with the authorities in this matter."

"Does this mean the roadblocks will be removed?" Jedidiah asked eagerly.

The chairman thought for a moment, then said, "Considering all that land was purchased with railroad funds, I don't think we'll have any trouble with the courts transferring the deeds to you... at the same price we paid for them, of course."

"Of course," Jedidiah said, laughing as he shook hands with the chairman of the board. For the first time since all this trouble had begun, Jedidiah felt a true sense of relief. He turned and looked at his friends. Matthew Colton whom he had known since childhood and Phineas B. Hargroves a man who had become a true ally, mentor, and friend. "I think

I can finally breathe!" he exclaimed.

Matthew clapped Jedidiah on the back, a broad grin spreading across his face in shared relief. "You and me both, Jed. You and me both."

Phineas, with his usual flair for dramatics, raised his hands in the air, "Gentlemen, to a hard-fought victory and the dawn of a new era!"

The three men shared a hearty laugh, the weight of their past struggles momentarily lifted by the promise of a brighter future ahead. They exchanged a series of firm handshakes with the board members, their faces alight with the satisfaction of resolution and justice served.

After being assured the railroad would be using the land they originally voted on and not the Davenport ranch, the trio made their way out of the headquarters, their strides resonant with the echoes of their recent triumph. As they exited the building, they squinted in the bright light of day, reflecting on the morning's unexpected turn of events. The workers bustled around them, unaware of the pivotal decisions that had just been made within the walls of the D.&R.W. Railroad headquarters.

As they approached the field where the Icarus had landed, the airship stood majestic and ready, basking in the sun's warm glow. Jedidiah led the way, with Matthew and Phineas following closely behind, their faces etched with contentment and relief.

"My ship truly is a beauty," Phineas remarked with a tinge of pride, admiring his creation that had carried them swiftly and safely to their destination.

Jedidiah and Matthew assisted Phineas aboard, ensuring he was comfortably settled. Climbing into the pilot's seat, Jedidiah felt a familiar sense of control and anticipation. He fired up the engines, the familiar hum, and hiss filling the air as the airship's heart came to life.

The Icarus rose gracefully, ascending above the rooftops of the D.&R.W. Railroad. Below them, the landscape unfurled like a patchwork quilt, the scenes of their recent endeavors growing smaller as they soared homeward.

"Let's go home," Jedidiah announced, a smile playing on his lips as he navigated the airship toward the vast expanse of his land.

Not even thirty minutes later, the Icarus descended gracefully, its shadow growing over the sprawling fields of the Davenport Ranch. As it touched down next to the reconverted hay barn, housing Jedidiah's airship, the engines quieted to a gentle purr before silencing completely. Jedidiah and Matthew offered assistance to Phineas, but he insisted that he didn't need any help.

"I've spent so much time working on your ship," Phineas declared, his eyes scanning the controls of the Icarus fondly. "I'd like to stay a little while and work on mine. A few tweaks here and there, you know."

Jedidiah nodded, understanding the inventor's attachment to his creation. "Take your time, Phineas. We'll be at my house deciding our next move."

Matthew and Jedidiah strolled away, their boots crunching against the dry grass. They approached their horses. They had been left grazing peacefully next to Jedidiah's buggy. Mounting with an ease born of years of experience, they paused to exchange a glance.

As they prepared to ride off, an unexpected threat loomed aboard the Icarus. As Phineas B. Hargroves was occupied toying with his ship, a shadowy figure was slowly creeping up behind him. Elijah Perkins, bruised from his leap and desperate, had somehow snuck aboard and stowed away unnoticed. With a revolver in hand, he emerged from his hiding spot, pointing the weapon at the unsuspecting Phineas.

"Start this thing up, Hargroves!" Perkins barked, his voice ragged with urgency and fear. "Now!"

Phineas, startled but composed, faced Perkins. His mind raced, calculating the risks and possibilities of this dire situation. Reluctantly, he moved to restart the airship, his hands steady despite the danger.

Outside, Jedidiah and Matthew, oblivious to the

unfolding drama, were about to guide their horses away, when a sudden commotion caught their attention. The familiar hum of the Icarus' steam engines starting up again was unmistakable. They exchanged a quick, puzzled look before Jedidiah's expression hardened.

"That's not right," Jedidiah muttered, urgency lacing his voice. He spurred his horse back towards the airship, with Matthew close behind. Their eyes were fixed on the ascending vessel, its silhouette growing smaller against the vast sky.

Rounding the end of the hangar, they saw Phineas at the controls with another man behind him – unmistakably Elijah Perkins. The sight of Perkins, with a gun at Phineas' back, sent a jolt of shock and anger through Jedidiah.

"Perkins!" Jedidiah shouted, his voice echoing across the fields, though it was too late. The Icarus, with its unwilling pilot and desperate stowaway, was already gaining altitude, drifting away from the ranch.

Matthew reined in his horse next to Jedidiah, his face etched with worry. "What's he doing with Phineas?"

Jedidiah clenched his fists, his eyes never leaving the shrinking airship. "He's taken Phineas hostage. We need to act fast."

They watched helplessly as the Icarus turned into a speck in the distance, carrying Phineas and his captor into the unknown. The immediate joy of their victory soured into concern and uncertainty.

"We need to get help," Matthew said, breaking the heavy silence. "We can't let Perkins get away with this."

Jedidiah nodded, his jaw set in determination. "We'll get Phineas back, and we'll bring Perkins to justice. This isn't over yet."

As the airship vanished from view, Jedidiah leaped from his horse. "I'm gonna open the roof and prepare the Phoenix for pursuit," Jedidiah declared. "Matt, you ride to the bunkhouse, find Jim, and have him round up some of the boys to follow on horseback!"

Matthew turned his horse and started galloping towards the bunkhouse. They needed to devise a plan – and quickly.

"I'll pick you up!" Jedidiah called out. He planned for Matthew Colton to go with him.

Dust kicked up under the horse's hooves, as Matthew raced towards the bunkhouse. The urgency of the situation was clear – every second counted.

Meanwhile, Jedidiah sprinted inside the hangar, his heart pounding in his chest. The Phoenix, his airship, stood ready, a beacon of hope in their pursuit of Perkins and the rescue of Phineas. He worked quickly to activate the steam engine that controlled the roof. With a series of clanks and hisses, the roof of the hangar began to slide open, revealing the expanse of the clear blue sky.

He climbed aboard the Phoenix, his movements swift and practiced. Turning the ignition, the engines roared to life, a powerful symphony of gears and steam. The airship began to lift, its propellers cutting through the air with increasing speed.

Arriving at the bunkhouse, Matthew found Jim Davis and several of the ranch hands already gathered together. "Perkins has taken Phineas hostage on the Icarus," he explained hurriedly. "We're going after them. Jed's in the air. We need to follow on the ground. Grab your rifles, and let's move!"

The men wasted no time. They saddled their horses and armed themselves, a determined look on each of their faces. They knew the land well, and if anyone could track Perkins and the Icarus from the ground, it was them.

Before Matthew could remount his horse he spotted the Phoenix hovering above them. Jedidiah lowered it just enough to throw a rope ladder over the side and motion for Colton to climb up. Once he was aboard, the airship started gaining altitude.

As the Phoenix soared into the sky, Jedidiah set a course following the last known direction of the Icarus. His eyes scanned the horizon, searching for any sign of the airship against the vast sky. Below him, Jim Davis and the ranch hands spread out, galloping across the landscape, their eyes sharp for any trace of the airship or any sign of where Perkins might be heading.

Jedidiah's grip on the controls was firm, his resolve unshaken. He knew the stakes were high – Phineas' life was in danger, and Perkins was desperate. But he also knew he wasn't alone in this fight. With him in the air, Matthew by his side, and the men on the ground, they formed a formidable team. The chase was on!

High above the sprawling landscapes of the Davenport Ranch, the Phoenix, piloted by Jedidiah, soared through the skies, its engines roaring with determination. Beside him, Matthew gripped the edges of the railing, his eyes scanning the horizon for any sign of the Icarus. Below, the ranch hands galloped across the fields, a cloud of dust trailing behind them.

"There!" Jedidiah pointed ahead, where the silhouette of the Icarus could be seen cruising at a surprisingly leisurely pace. It seemed Phineas, despite the peril he was in, was using his wits to give them a fighting chance.

Matthew squinted, trying to make out the details. "He's keeping it slow. Smart move, Phineas."

Jedidiah nodded, a plan forming in his mind. "I'm going to hover above them. Matthew, I need you to take the controls."

"Okay, I'll take the..." Matthew's eyes widened in alarm. "I'll take the what?"

"Just keep it steady," Jedidiah said, preparing to lower the Phoenix's ladder.

"I've never piloted an airship before!" Matthew shouted in vain, as he watched his friend ignore him and continue as though he wasn't even speaking. "I've never even touched the controls!"

"You've got this!" Jedidiah positioned the ladder directly above the Icarus' airbag. He glanced down, gauging the distance and wind. With a deep breath, he began his precarious descent, the ladder swaying gently beneath him.

Matthew, with a white-knuckled grip, tried to keep the Phoenix as steady as possible, muttering to himself about never signing up for airship piloting.

Jedidiah stepped down onto the top of the Icarus' airbag and immediately dropped down his hands and knees. He carefully maneuvered across its surface. He could barely make out the sounds of Perkins' voice as he berated Phineas below him.

He prepared himself to climb down the side. Just as he was about to make his move, a sudden gust of wind caused the Icarus to sway. Jedidiah tightened his grip on the cables surrounding the airbag and hung on for dear life. He waited for the right moment. After the wind had settled down,

Jedidiah shimmied down the cables and stealthily dropped down on the deck of the ship.

He silently made his way towards Perkins and Hargroves. The former railroad executive had his back to him and never heard him coming. With a burst of energy, Jedidiah launched himself into a flying tackle, catching Perkins completely off guard.

The two men tumbled across the cabin floor, Perkins' gun skittering away. Phineas, seizing the moment, ran after the gun, ready to assist. But Jedidiah had everything under control, pinning Perkins down with a determined glare.

"You're not getting away this time, Perkins," Jedidiah growled.

Matthew, above in the Phoenix, continued to hold his breath not realizing the fight below him was over and Perkins was securely in Jedidiah's grasp.

Back on the ground, the ranch hands who had been following the chase could only marvel at the sight of the two airships, one hovering above the other in a remarkable display of aerial mastery.

Leveling the gun at his kidnapper, Phineas told Jedidiah to check the chest in his cabin for a pair of handcuffs.

"Why do you have handcuffs?" Jedidiah asked with a puzzled look on his face.

Hargroves merely laughed as he replied, "My

dear boy, I've told you before, it's best to be prepared!"

After guiding the Icarus to a smooth landing on the ground, where Jim Davis and the other ranch hands awaited, Jedidiah Davenport and Phineas B. Hargroves stepped out with a sense of triumph. Between them, they firmly escorted the captive Elijah Perkins, his anger evident but futile. With a nod to Jim and the men, they handed over Perkins, entrusting them to deliver the disgraced man to the custody of Sheriff Thompson in town.

As the two men watched the group ride away, Phineas glanced up at the sky and spotted the Phoenix still hovering in the same spot. "My dear boy, who is flying your ship?"

"Oh, that's..." Jedidiah suddenly cut his sentence short. His eyes widened and his face drained of color. A sudden realization struck him as he glanced up at the sky. The only way back to his airship was to mirror the precarious maneuver he had just executed to board the Icarus. He turned to Phineas Hargroves. "How long can an airship hover before it begins losing altitude?"

****

Later that night, after Elijah Perkins was safely behind bars and both airships had been stowed neatly away, everyone on the ranch gathered around a campfire to celebrate. The air was filled with the smell of a sumptuous feast, the work of both Pat Bennington, Jedidiah's chef, and Leo Green, the cook for the ranch hands. Their combined efforts resulted in a spread that was both hearty and delicious, perfectly suited for the occasion.

Sheriff Thompson and most of the business leaders of Spoon Fork were present, having been invited to celebrate the hard-fought victory. Among the attendees were key figures such as Luther Caldwell, Jacob Harrington, Horace McKinley, Henry Porter, and Gideon Stewart.

Sheriff Thompson, usually a figure of authority and sternness, seemed more relaxed tonight, his laughter mingling with the lively conversations. He approached Jedidiah, clapping him on the shoulder with a grin. "Jed, I must say, I didn't know how you were gonna pull this off. That was some chase!"

Jedidiah laughed in response, "Sheriff, I couldn't have done it without your support. And, of course, Phineas and Matthew here," he said, gesturing to his companions.

Glancing intently at his mentor, a thought suddenly came to him. "Phineas," Jedidiah began, with a mischievous glint in his eye, "don't you think it's time you told us the whole story about those men who were chasing you in Wichita?"

Matthew nodded in agreement, leaning in.

"Yeah, you've kept us in the dark long enough."

Phineas chuckled, his eyes twinkling in the warm glow of the firelight. He took a sip of his drink, savoring the moment. "My dear boys," he started, with a dramatic pause, "I promise I'll tell you the whole tale one of these days. But for now, let me sum it up in three words... Myra Wilhelmina Bancroft."

Jedidiah and Matthew exchanged a knowing glance, their expressions a mix of surprise, intrigue, and puzzlement. "Myra Wilhelmina Bancroft!" they exclaimed in unison.

Myra Wilhelmina Bancroft was a legend among adventurers and treasure hunters. Known for her fearless spirit and keen intellect. She was the captain of her airship, the Enigma. Myra's exploits were legendary, from uncovering lost cities to outsmarting the most cunning of rivals. With a sharp wit and a keen eye for detail, she was as skilled in negotiation as she was in navigating the skies. Her tales were as numerous as the stars, each adventure more thrilling than the last.

Neither Jedidiah Davenport nor Matthew Colton could figure out how she played into Hargrove's story but admitted it could wait for another day. Jedidiah turned to his housekeeper, Agatha Porter, and asked her what she thought about how everything turned out.

The older woman, standing next to fellow

servant Pat Bennington, smiled and replied, "Things worked out so well, I don't even mind putting up with you know who tonight." She elbowed the portly man teasingly in the ribs.

"Land o' Goshen!" Pat's face started to turn red as he blushed with embarrassment. "Well, Jed, what are you going to do with with all the money from that oil well of yours?"

"Start building my fleet!" Jedidiah declared, determined.

"Fleet?" Pat asked confused.

"Fleet of airships!" The young entrepreneur motioned in the general direction of where the men would soon be laying the railroad tracks. "With this new iron horse galloping through the valley, we must be ready for a new kind of battle. To keep my freight business not just surviving, but thriving, we need to soar higher and faster."

A sense of anticipation hung in the air. It was clear that this was not the end of his adventures but rather a new beginning, a leap into an even grander venture.

The adventures of Jedidiah Davenport will continue! Be sure to join us in *Sky Races* A Jedidiah Davenport Adventure. Follow Jedidiah as he takes to the skies once again. What new challenges will he face? What mysteries will unfold in the clouds? Find out in the next thrilling installment of Jedidiah's saga!

Current titles in the
Jedidiah Davenport Adventure Series

Coming March 2025
Quest for the Lost Relic